The bathroom was enveloped in steam. Cool air displaced the mist when Helen opened the door. Frieda's body was shown in vague outline on the frosted glass of the shower door. Helen watched the soap bubble and froth on her dark skin, dissolving under the rhythmic, circular motions of her hands. The water swirled out from her head as she flung her hair from her eyes and arched her back to rinse the soap from the dark loose strands. With each upward movement of her arms, her breasts lifted, gleaming in the water. Helen no longer felt pain in her hand when she opened the shower door and slipped inside.

"How about some company?"

"I thought you'd never ask." Frieda moved away from the stream of water, allowing Helen to stand under the shower head. "Is your hand okay? Does that cut hurt?"

"What cut?"

Frieda worked the soap into a thick lather while Helen stood still under her hands. She lingered on her breasts, kneading, massaging warmth into them. One hand slipped between her legs and repeated the slow, smooth motion. Helen felt a moan well up in the back of her throat.

"Not yet. Not here."

About the Author

Pat Welch lives in the San Francisco Bay area. Her mysteries include *Murder By the Book, Still Waters, Proper Burial,* and coming in 1995, *Open House.*

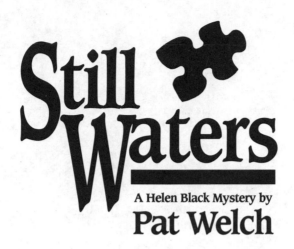

Still Waters

A Helen Black Mystery by
Pat Welch

The Naiad Press, Inc.
1994

Printed in the United States of America on acid-free paper
First Edition
Second Printing March, 1994

Edited by Claire McNab and Katherine V. Forrest
Cover design by Pat Tong and Bonnie Liss
    (Phoenix Graphics)
Typeset by Sandi Stancil

Library of Congress Cataloging-in-Publication Data

Welch, Pat, 1957–
    Still waters: a Helen Black mystery / by Pat Welch.
        p.   cm.
    ISBN 0-941483-97-5
    I. Title.
PS3573.E4543S7   1991
813'.54—dc20   91-24004
                                                    CIP

For my family

Acknowledgments

Many thanks to Katherine V. Forrest, Claire McNab, and Barbara Grier for all their help.

Chapter One

Jill Gallagher looked up into the bathroom mirror and saw her own twisted features staring back at her. Red-rimmed eyes, bleary from lack of sleep, blinked in the harsh light of the bare bulb poking out from the stained wallpaper above the mirror. She leaned forward, rubbed at the strange image with its crooked eyes, broken nose, and grimacing lips. She couldn't be that drunk yet — too early. No, no, it was a flaw in the mirror, one of those wavy ridges that distorted whatever it reflected. Like the funhouse at the fair. Jill shook her head slowly, trying to laugh off her sudden case of the jitters. A cigarette would help. She burrowed through the huge bag she always carried with her. Combs, pens, torn scraps of paper, an odd coin or two flew in the vicinity of the sink until she remembered she'd given up smoking for the millionth time only last week.

"Fuck," she mumbled as she jammed everything back in the bag. One last look at the wallet yielded no hidden treasures. With a sigh she zipped her bag, caught a glimpse of her crazy face in the warped mirror, and then ran her stubby hands through her short, thick blonde hair, trying not to notice the dark roots that threatened near her scalp. Hell, she'd let herself go these last few weeks. Well, who could blame her?

"Come on, lady, you been in there for an hour! Other people gotta go, you know!" The high-pitched voice whined through the door at Jill, cutting short her thoughts. She slung the bag over her shoulder and opened the door. The noise from the bar blasted her senses as she shouldered her way past the woman who'd been waiting for her to emerge.

Jill stood silent for a moment, leaning against the door, waiting. Soon she was able to make out shapes through the thick smoke. Cowboy hats towered in the distance as their wearers awkwardly danced their newly learned two-steps across the sawdust that had been spread across the floor a few hours ago. The rich tones of Johnny Cash gave way to the tinny bleat of someone Jill couldn't identify as she squeezed past the clusters of people back to the bar. Mercifully there was a vacant stool before her, and she sank down with relief.

"Time for another one, hon?" The burly bartender

leaned in front of her, his belly unashamedly wedging up against the bar. Although the plaid shirt and "howdy-ma'am" accents of his speech were all quite correct, Jill doubted that the pale flabby hands splayed on the polished wood had ever roped a steer or branded a hide.

"How the hell did someone with a name like Sidney get a job at a place called the Lame Duck Saloon?" Jill asked, stalling for time as she groped once more into her empty wallet.

Sidney smiled patiently. "Just lucky, I guess."

Jill gave up. "I don't suppose you'd cash another check for me, would you?"

"Hell, no! Not after that last one you gave me bounced sky-high. My boss gave me hell over that one. Now don't be looking at me like that, I just can't. You know that. 'Sides, I thought hotshot reporters made lots of money."

"All right, all right." Jill drummed her fingers on the counter. "Coffee still on the house?"

"You bet. And I won't even charge you for the napkin."

A moment later a white mug appeared before her. Jill picked it up, her fingers covering the crude sketch of a duck wearing a cowboy hat, bandanna, and stupid grin. The coffee tasted like shit, but it settled her nerves. She sat this way for some time, thinking hard, ignoring the looks thrown her way by some of the men who circled the bar like predators. She reached for her bag once again, hesitated, then opened it quickly and started rummaging. Her search resulted in a handful of coins — enough for a couple of phone calls.

"Sidney! Hey, Sid!" He heard her shout, nodded,

3

and sauntered back over to her. "Do you have a yellow pages here?" she asked.

The thick black eyebrows lifted in surprise. "Yellow pages? Yeah, I think so." He searched under the bar. "Calling up your boyfriend?" he asked as he slapped the volume down in front of her.

"No, my shrink," she retorted, suddenly sick to death of this horrible bar full of Sidneys — weak urban cowboys who'd probably run screaming into the night if they ever caught sight of a horse.

Sidney apparently chose not to be offended at her tone and laughed heartily at her humor. He walked away as her eager hands found the listing she wanted. Scooping the coins into her palm, she swiveled off the stool. A glance into the narrow hall that held two phones decided her on the gas station across the road. With a final curse for having to leave her car back in the woods, Jill went outside.

As she crossed the two-lane asphalt to the gas station, Jill had no eyes for the masses of stars sprayed across the black sky over the Berkeley hills. The clock, dimly glowing behind the glass expanse of the office, showed eleven o'clock. Jill eased the phone booth door almost shut, preventing the light from announcing her presence to cars passing by. Even as she dropped coins into the slot and waited for the dial tone, she knew this was foolish. Just because her old buddy Helen Black had become a successful private eye didn't mean she would be slaving away at the office at this late hour. Helen was probably at home in bed with that rather delicious woman, the artist, doing some very private investigation.

Jill nearly hung up when she heard the inevitable response of an answering machine.

4

Instead, she held onto the receiver and waited for the beep. "Why the hell am I acting like this?" she muttered at herself, trying to smile. One look at her pale strained face, reflected in the glass of the booth, told her. Unlike the mirror in the bar's bathroom, this surface told no jokes, no lies. Jill saw the hunched over shoulders, the tall thin body stiff with tension. Her big dark eyes provided a startling contrast to her disheveled blonde hair that had been pushed about by nervous hands. "I am scared to death," she whispered.

Then the beep sounded. Jill lowered her head and spoke rapidly, unaware that other eyes were watching her every move. They saw her hang up, lean against the back of the booth and take a deep breath.

With a sudden jerking movement she stepped out of the booth, then hesitated. Back to the bar? No. She started walking rapidly in the opposite direction, down the empty road. The figure hiding in the shadows by the gas station waited until Jill's footsteps on the pavement had nearly faded away.

Jill walked rapidly, almost running, skirting the highway on the right. To her left the sounds of the Lame Duck Saloon were deadened by the evergreens that had somehow managed to survive years of drought. As soon as she'd passed by the gas station, Jill could hear on her right the faint, unmistakable sound of water lapping up on a shore. Still Waters Lake moved gently, stirred by the breeze filtering in over the hills from San Francisco Bay. Jill instinctively put out one hand for guidance and her fingers clasped the cold metal railing that protected her from the sheer drop of three hundred feet to the water's edge. A car sped by, horn blaring and brights flashing. Her heart pounding, Jill stopped, grabbing the railing with both hands. This was too close to the road. Some drunken fool would run her down. Fortunately the path leading up to her destination veered away from the road. Her feet found the well-worn trail just as her eyes saw the huge sign looming up below a dim street lamp. STILL WATERS LODGE welcomed her in big letters painted to look like logs. Jill almost laughed out loud in her relief. She was nearly home.

It was just as her hands left the railing that the blow fell. There was only a sharp, dazzling pain, then blankness.

Jill's body hit once against the rocks, then fell just at the point where water met a thin ring of white sand. The contents of the bag, so carefully collected only minutes before, were scattered for several yards on rock and water. No cars moved by on the road. Only the moon, remote and white over the lake, bore witness to the alien shape that had been flung onto the sand.

Chapter Two

Frieda reached out for the newspaper, her eyes searching Helen's face as she did so. No tears were visible, although Helen had just read aloud an account of the death of an old friend. "I just can't believe it," Frieda said softly as she read over the article. "We haven't heard anything from Jill Gallagher for — what is it now, a couple of years?"

"Almost exactly two years ago." Helen got up from the table and turned her back on the remains of breakfast.

On Sunday mornings since they'd moved into

their new apartment on Russell Street Helen had volunteered to cook — a task she hated at any other time. Now she was glad of the excuse to prowl around the kitchen, moving from table to sink and back again, camouflaging her feelings by gathering plates. Out of the corner of her eye she saw Frieda's thin frame sink into one of the lopsided chairs they'd picked up at a garage sale. Helen opened the refrigerator door to put away the orange juice and felt a cool shaft of air stroke her flushed cheeks. At her feet, Boobella moaned a weak feline plea and pawed at the laces of her tennis shoes.

Frieda broke the silence. "It says she fell down a cliff into a lake. I had no idea there was a lake out there. Where is this place — Still Waters Lodge — anyway?"

Helen risked a glance at her lover's face, which was shielded by long brown hair that fell forward over the newspaper. "It's up in those hills between Berkeley and Orinda. Some kind of man-made lake. It was supposed to be a reservoir when they started out, but I guess the county ran out of money. Developers got hold of it and turned it into a sort of resort thing."

"That's the last place on earth Jill would want to be, from what I can remember of her. But I didn't know her as well as you did."

Helen shrugged, clattered the last dish into the sink, turned on the tap. "She sort of took me under her wing when I first came out here from Mississippi. If it hadn't been for her and Aunt Josephine, I know I wouldn't have survived." The dishes tumbling in the sink hid the tremor in her voice. "She was a damned good reporter, too, in spite of what everyone said. If she'd just stayed away from the booze . . ." Helen let the sentence go unfinished and swabbed savagely at a frying pan.

"Is that why they fired her from the *Chronicle*?" Frieda asked, getting up from the table and moving closer to the sink.

"I don't know. That was right after the three of us had dinner two years ago. She would never tell me anything about it — just laughed, pretended it didn't matter."

"But I'm sure it did." Suddenly Frieda's hands were on Helen's shoulders, kneading the tension. "Honey, why don't you let me do those today? Take a Sunday off from kitchen duty."

"No, I'm fine." Frieda's hands stayed where they were, but Helen was rigid. "Really, I'll be all right. Don't worry about me."

Frieda moved to one side and leaned against the counter, one hand caressing Helen's arm. "I guess we'll never know exactly what happened. The story in the paper implies it was an accident."

Helen froze for a moment at the sink, then dried her hands on a towel. "Frieda, sit down."

"What? What is it?"

"There's something I want you to hear." Helen stepped carefully over the cat and rummaged in the backpack she used as a briefcase. Frieda watched as Helen fingered a thin wedge of black plastic. It was a small cassette. Helen placed it into the dusty tape player that sat neglected by the window. With her eyes averted from Frieda, Helen sat down to listen.

The familiar voice boomed out over the kitchen. They both jumped, and Helen reached out to adjust the sound. "*Remember me, Helen? It's your old*

9

drinking buddy, Jill. Bet you're surprised to hear from me after all this time." There was a nervous laugh, followed by a strange rushing sound — wind, perhaps? "It's Friday night, well actually almost Saturday. I'm staying at this hotel, and — well, it's kind of a long story. I think I'm in need of your services. Professionally, I mean. Someone's been following me." The laugh surfaced again. "Sounds crazy, doesn't it? But I have proof this time — proof that will make those macho assholes at the Chronicle sorry for what they did. I've just spent the last half hour hiding it. Give me a call at Still Waters Lodge, room two-twenty-four. As soon as you can. Oh — and tell that delicious woman I said hi. Bye for now."

The tape whirred to a stop, rewound itself, and the machine snapped into silence. Frieda was quiet, waiting for Helen to speak. "I heard that late last night, when I stopped by the office to get my backpack. There was some paperwork I wanted to do this afternoon. I listened to this just before I left."

"Did you try to call her last night? At the hotel?"

"Yes, I did. They kept ringing her room, but there was no answer. The body wasn't discovered, according to the paper, until last night. I'm sure she must have been dead by the time I heard this." Abruptly, Helen got up and removed the cassette from the machine. "She says someone is following her, then she turns up dead. Don't even say it, Frieda."

"I wasn't going to say anything."

"But I can hear you thinking. The same thoughts occurred to me — that Jill was positive she was a dyke version of Brenda Starr, that she'd finally taken one drink too many, that she had paranoid delusions of grandeur. Who the hell would want to follow a has-been reporter with a drinking problem?"

"Hey, calm down! I'm not the enemy."

"I know. Sorry," Helen mumbled. She stood by the window, her fingernails tapping on the cassette. Outside, a group of children ran down Russell Street heading for the playground on Martin Luther King Drive. The day was cold and windy, with a hint of rain in the air. Weak rays of sunlight were beginning to seep through the gray sky, but they were threatened by the thickening clouds. "I hate this time of year. Seems like summer will never come. Who said April was the cruelest month? I think it was in a poem."

"Helen, what are you going to do about that tape?"

"I already made a copy of it for the police. I'm taking it over later."

"Good. Now, why do I get the feeling there's something you're not telling me?" Frieda came and stood by her, one arm around her shoulders, a hand gently turning Helen's face toward her own. "What is it?"

"I'm going to call the hotel later and make reservations for a few days." She moved away from Frieda's embrace and headed back to the sink. "You can get mad at me if you want, but I'm doing it. I have to find out for myself what happened."

"So who's mad? Look, I know I haven't always been as supportive as you'd like about your detective agency —"

"That's the understatement of the year." The water was cold. Helen, in a sudden fit of anger, threw the sopping dishrag into the water and leaned with both hands against the counter. "We've practically started divorce proceedings once or twice over this, if you recall."

Frieda stayed by the window, arms folded across her chest. "Yes, I know, Helen. But this time it's a little different. Jill was your friend — our friend. Maybe we'll find out it was an accident, maybe we won't. But we have to do something.

"*We?* What's this *we?*"

"I'd like to go with you to the hotel." Helen turned around to see Frieda's face, its thin, worried features set in grim determination. "Before you say no, just think about it."

"But you have that exhibit coming up at the University. You can't really take time away from that. It's too important."

"So I'll go over for a while today and finish things up at the studio. Then I can take a few days off and be with you at the hotel." Helen felt a familiar sense of panic fluttering into her stomach as Frieda added, "Don't you want me to go?"

"It's not that, sweetheart," she managed to stammer. "I don't think you know what's involved. I have to ask questions, poke and pry — generally make a lot of people very uncomfortable. I'm not sure you should go along for the ride."

"No? Well, I'm sure. It's about time I got a chance to see what you do for a living."

"Why all of a sudden —"

"Because of who died," Frieda interrupted. "I want to know what happened to Jill just as much as you do." She walked swiftly across the room and

12

hugged Helen tight. "I'm sorry, so sorry, that she's dead."

"I'm sorry, too." As Frieda backed off and held her at arms' length, Helen said, "You go on over to the studio. I'll finish up here and take that tape to the police."

"I can go to the studio any time. Why don't I stay here with you and we'll take the tape together?"

"Don't worry so much! I'm all right. See? I'm not screaming in agony or falling apart or anything."

"I know. That's what worries me. Underneath that strong silent exterior you must be in a lot of pain. And you don't want me to see that, not even after all the time we've been together." Frieda let her go with a sigh. "All right. I'm going to go to the studio for a while. We'll talk some more about this when I get back."

"Thanks, Frieda."

"For what?"

"For putting up with me."

Helen busied herself at the sink until she heard her lover's car grinding its ancient gears out of the carport onto the street. Fresh hot water splashed over the plates, mixing with the tears Helen no longer tried to stifle. Her aching eyes stared at the calendar above the sink without seeing the rows of numbered days. In her mind it was October — six months earlier — and she was standing in the middle of Jill Gallagher's apartment.

Jill herself was in the bathroom. Helen waited, trying not to notice the squalor all around. Newspapers and magazines were scattered across the dirty rug as if thrown there, and cups and glasses with stale sediment dotted the furniture. Cobwebs floated from the corners of the ceiling. Surveying the scene with distaste, Helen nearly knocked down a small vase from the mantel, as Jill returned. "Hey, be careful with the goods!" Jill laughed.

"Sorry." Helen steadied the vase back to a safe position, glad of the chance to look away from Jill. She had donned a slinky black robe that flapped loose over her breasts. The slit on the side revealed legs that were still tanned and shapely.

"I don't think it's cracked," Helen said.

"It better not be. It has great sentimental value," Jill intoned with mocking wide eyes. "A gift from a sweet young thing who finds me irresistible."

"You were never short on those."

"All except you, Tex. I could never coax you to try a little forbidden fruit with me."

Helen laughed in spite of herself. "You know damn well I'm from Mississippi, not Texas."

"Same thing." Jill sank onto the sofa with a sigh, sweeping a couple of paper plates onto the floor. "Have a seat."

Helen sat down gingerly. "I got your note," she said, pulling a slip of paper from her coat pocket. "I'm sorry I missed you yesterday."

"It's really not fair, forcing me to be so indiscreet, leaving notes on your door. What would Frieda say about that?"

"Nothing, since she never goes there."

"I like Frieda. A little thin for my taste, but very sweet." Jill took a deep drag on her cigarette, then started to cough. Helen waited for the paroxysm to end.

14

"You said in the note you had to see me. What's wrong?"

Jill tossed her head back and attempted a throaty laugh. "Same old Helen. No time for the amenities."

"If there's anything I can do —"

"Just take a look around you, honey. The best thing you could do for me is shoot me, put me out of my misery." Jill stretched out a leg and kicked at one of the stacks of newspapers. "I'm reduced to writing up dog and pony shows for suburban weeklies, did you know that? Real Pulitzer Prize material."

Helen had listened to Jill for several minutes before she realized that the woman was working up to a request for money. It wouldn't be the first time, nor the last, Helen was sure.

This time Jill made only the barest pretense of refusal before taking the bills. "To do this up right I ought to have a garter on my thigh — you know, like in some Marlene Dietrich movie."

Helen made a fuss over buttoning up her coat to cover her embarrassment, then looked up to find Jill's eyes, red-rimmed and shot with yellow, staring at her knowingly. "You know I'll always help you when I can, Jill," she said as she placed a hand on the door knob.

"As long as the little woman at home doesn't know about it, you mean."

"Frieda would never object to this. Anyway this is between you and me. It always has been."

Jill moved closer, and Helen could smell the bourbon odor move with her. "There was a time when you wanted me, Tex," she breathed. "Remember? When I showed you the ropes? We were together every chance we got."

"Of course I remember," Helen said, forcing a smile. "How could I forget?"

Jill turned away with a laugh. "You'd be surprised what people forget. Thanks, Helen. I'll pay you back someday. Maybe I'll send a rich client to your office one of these days."

"I could always use one of those." Helen was out the door and virtually running down the hall to the stairs before Jill could say another word.

The sound of her own feet pounding on the cement of the stairs faded in her memory as she realized the dishwater in the sink had grown cold around her wrists. Her own tears, pelting the cold suds, fixed her thoughts back on the present. She wiped her wet cheeks and started the dishes again.

Chapter Three

The door to the Lame Duck Saloon was locked. Helen glanced down at her watch. Only ten-thirty. She'd come back this way after lunch, try to rustle up someone who might have seen Jill. She made her noisy way across the gravel back to the car where Frieda waited. Frieda rolled down the window as she approached.

"Nobody's home," Helen said, leaning against the car door. "Too early, I think." She squinted across the road. "I can't believe the difference in weather between here and Berkeley. We were driving through fog and drizzle just on the other side of the Caldecott Tunnels."

"I know! I love it," Frieda said with a big smile, turning her face to take in the sunlight that streamed through the windshield. "It's like being in another part of the world."

Helen snorted. "You can say that again. Just try talking to the police here. I always hated working with them when I was a cop."

"Well, they did take the tape and listen to it. I mean, at least they took you seriously."

"They practically patted me on the head and told me to go back home and play with my Barbie and Skipper dream house."

Frieda frowned and tapped her fingers on the steering wheel. Behind them a huge eighteen-wheeler chugged up the road, straining at the steep incline. Once it had passed, Frieda asked, "Can't your ex-partner do anything to help?"

"I can't bother Manny with something like this. I'm just working on hunches now. I don't even have a client. There's nothing he could do at this point."

"Well, let's go on and get registered at the hotel. We can come back later." Frieda reached over to open the passenger door, then looked back in surprise when Helen took a couple of steps away from the car. "Aren't you coming?"

"I'll follow you. I'd like to take a walk up the road, try to check out the area a bit."

"Right." Still Frieda waited. "Want any help?"

Helen looked down at her and smiled. "You already help me more than you know. Just by caring enough to come along."

"At your service." The tone was light, even

18

mocking, but Helen could see that Frieda was touched by the sudden, rare moment of tenderness. Helen squeezed Frieda's hand briefly before watching her drive off in a whirl of dust and gravel. Then she silently cursed herself for her own inability to scale the dark barriers between them. What was it that made her shy away from intimacy?

She stood in the parking lot brooding until the roar of another truck brought her back to the present. As she crossed the grimy concrete toward a gas station, avoiding the worst greasy puddles, she recalled Jill's final message. The background noise picked up by the tape had been virtually nil — no indication that loud, hilarious drinking was happening a few feet away. Perhaps Jill had been in a public phone booth. The strange rushing sound might have been a passing car.

"Can I help you with somethin'?" Helen was startled from her thoughts by a young man, about fourteen, whose grease-smeared face and hands bore witness to his occupation. His steady gaze held a gleam of curiosity and Helen realized he must have seen her wandering around the bar across the road.

"Is there a phone here?"

He waved a smudged towel. "Right around the side of the building." He took a few steps along with her. "You're not a cop, are you?"

Helen suppressed a smile. "No, I'm not. Why, do I look like one?"

He shrugged. "I dunno. We just had a lot of 'em around lately. Lots of questions." He jerked his head back toward the road. "I seen you over at the saloon."

"They weren't open."

19

"The owner usually shows up around noon." He leaned against the wall and continued wiping his hands on the rag in a useless effort to get them clean. "You're here about that woman that fell down into the lake, aren't you? You a reporter?"

Helen shook her head. "Just a friend of hers." She felt a pang at the irony — only her death could make Jill newsworthy again. "I'm just sort of wondering how it all happened."

"Oh. Yeah. Sorry. About your friend, I mean." He hung his head in mock solemnity, but Helen could see the eager gleam in his eye. And why not? Probably the only excitement this kid ever got around here was a messy oil change. "We was closed when it happened."

"What time was that?"

They were interrupted by a bellow from the depths of the garage. "Jim! Jim, you get back in here this minute! Mrs. Belden's coming over this morning for her Mercedes! Jim! Where the devil have you got to now?"

A huge man — an older, fatter version of Jim — emerged into the sunlight. He had Jim's light blue eyes, but in his case the years had layered fat around them. His belly jiggled as he sighed. "How many times have I got to tell you, boy, you're here to work?"

"I won't keep him long," Helen called out after seeing the plea in Jim's eyes. "My car's just a little way up the road, I was hoping he would just take a look under the hood." The man's face was unrelenting, so Helen decided to pad it a little. "My husband will murder me if he finds out I've done

20

something to his Porsche. He just worships that car — I always say he loves it more than he loves me."

Helen devoutly hoped she hadn't sounded too simpering, but Jim's father changed his demeanor dramatically at the mention of the car's make. Hearing the possible clink of money into his cash register, he beamed broadly and nodded. "You go on up with the lady, Jim," he sang out. "See what you can do. We got the truck ready if you need to tow it."

As they walked away from the garage, the road curved slightly to the left. Helen sensed that Jim was bursting to talk, but he waited until he was sure his father couldn't see them. He stopped abruptly at the edge of the railing Helen had spotted from the bar. "It was my friend, Bob," Jim said. "He saw her."

"The woman who died? Jill Gallagher?"

"Yeah, that's what the paper said her name was. Bob hauls lumber all hours, over to Orinda for a new development they're building out there. He comes down from Oregon with his haul and takes it right over so they can start early —"

Helen cut him short. "What exactly did he see?"

"Well, he says it was eleven o'clock. He was coming right past the garage —"

"What made him notice the time?"

" 'Cause he thought about stopping over at the Lame Duck for a drink. No beer or nothin' — just maybe a Coke. He's always real careful. Anyways, he saw how late it was and decided to go ahead and finish his run. Next thing he knows, this woman is right there, practically in the road. She only just

21

jumped out of his way in time. He could've killed her, you know?"

"I know." Helen looked at his eager, animated face. The death of a stranger, under mysterious circumstances, held no tragedy or pain for this boy — it was merely an excuse for leaving behind the dreary world of his father. "Did Bob tell the police?"

"Oh, yeah, sure! I went with him." Jim's face clouded. "Boy, did that piss off the old man. He gave me hell for that." He added in a confidential tone, "Bob figures the police think she was drunk, fallin' down from it."

"And what do you think, Jim?"

At that point Helen saw through the trees that Jim's father had walked a few yards up the road from the garage — no doubt expecting to see his son hurrying back for the tow truck. "Oh, God," Jim moaned. "Here he comes. I got to go."

"You won't get into trouble, will you?"

"Hell, no! I can handle the old man. You just better be sure to come back and finish talking to me, so you can get the story right for the paper."

Before Helen could respond, Jim had fled. Once alone, she was enveloped in silence. It was a lonely spot. Jim had led her to a narrow swath of grass just beyond a few straggly evergreen trees. The trees shielded her from the edge of the road, but it was a narrow margin of safety. Anyone wandering in this area in the dark would risk serious injury from passing cars or trucks.

The thought of Jill walking through this strip to her death gave rise to a question that had been bothering her, off and on, since she and Frieda had first driven up the road to the hotel. Where the hell had Jill's car been while all this was going on? Granted, it was only a short walk back to the hotel — no more than fifteen minutes — but Helen had never known a native of California who would walk when driving was an option. Besides, Jill had set off late at night. In the dark. Alone. Seeing the terrain Jill had had to cover, Helen felt certain that the location of the car was important.

Helen turned around, gripped the railing firmly with both hands, and looked down. She was unprepared for the sight of the rough surface of rock falling down three hundred feet to a strip of sand. The deep blue of the water contrasted impressively with the white face of the rock. A feeling of nausea threatened to overcome her. Christ almighty — Jill must have been a mess when she reached the bottom. Even at this distance Helen could see the jagged knife-sharp edges of gray stone.

To regain her composure Helen lifted her eyes to survey the lake. She hadn't expected to see such beauty here. What made the water so blue, she wondered. Although the sun shone warm and inviting, she knew the water must be quite cold. She couldn't make out swimmers, but there were several small boats floating in serene isolation across the smooth surface of the lake, all sporting at least one fishing pole, and she could see couples strolling hand in hand around the ring of white sand. Through a thickly wooded slope to her left, an unpaved trail led away from the sand and presumably up to the hotel. She'd have to explore that later, with Frieda.

Helen had a sudden cheerful image of Frieda enjoying the natural beauty of the lake, her long dark hair tossed into her eyes by the wind — then she stopped herself. This was not Berkeley, she reminded herself. This was no place for two women to be taking a romantic stroll on a beach. Besides, they were here for a specific reason. Feeling grimly determined, Helen turned her eyes back to the rocks below.

She felt herself going into the same emotional deep-freeze she'd used as a cop, shutting off everything with some mental switch. She looked down at the railing. It was at her waist, just high enough to provide leverage for someone determined to push a body over to fall to the rocks. Or, just enough to trip up a drunk, making her stumble to her death. She ran her hands over the cold metal, walking up and down its length, carefully testing its even surface. No indication of damage — everywhere her fingers found a smooth, cool patina.

Helen looked back at the trees. All intact there. If a car had run Jill down, wouldn't the signs have been obvious? Even investigators bent on finding an accident would not have ignored broken, battered trees and tire marks. If Jill had, in fact, been murdered, it was by someone on foot like Jill herself had been.

A cool wind reminded Helen that, in spite of the sunshine, it was still April. It ruffled along her scalp and sent shivers down her spine. Thoughts of Frieda and coffee — and even a shot of bourbon — got her feet into motion. As she walked back towards the road, she turned for one last look at the lake. It was then that she saw the figure moving on the gray rocks below.

Chapter Four

"You're sure it was a girl?" Frieda nestled back more comfortably into the wing chair. The lobby of Still Waters Lodge was empty except for the two women sitting near the registration desk.

Helen smiled. "Surely I can be trusted to make out the shape of a woman's body by now? It was female, and she was moving over those rocks like a mountain goat. She'd been there before."

"Well, what was she doing? I mean, was she looking for something?"

Helen shrugged. "Hard to say. She climbed off

the rocks and went back up to the path. She didn't see me."

As Frieda frowned over this piece of information, Helen surveyed the room. She didn't have a lot of experience in hotel lobbies, but this one was an odd mixture of rustic and genteel. A few old-fashioned wing chairs, like the one in which Frieda sat, dotted the floral-patterned carpet that had seen better times. The chairs provided a contrast to the vinyl covered sofas lining two of the walls. Interspersed among the furniture were brass tubs containing artificial greenery. To top it all off, broad wooden beams supported an arched ceiling. At the far end of the room an empty fireplace dominated the scene, as if staring blankly at the decorating nightmare.

"Could you recognize her again?" Frieda was asking when a commotion was heard outside.

Shadows played for a moment on the wooden steps that led from the wide front driveway up to the lobby. The heavy glass door flew open and banged against the wall. Two children, a boy and a girl, darted into the lobby, trailing a scent of suntan lotion and sweat.

"Bobby! Susie! Settle down, *now!*" The proprietary anger in the voice indicated parenthood. The children's mother stalked in on high heels. One taloned hand flashed red nails as she whipped at the face of the little boy. "If you keep it up I'll send you straight back to your room. No more going out on the lake today."

The boy she'd called Bobby put a grimy hand to his afflicted cheek and promptly began to whine. "But, Mom, I just wanted to see where that lady fell." His older sister rolled her eyes at such babyish

26

behavior and slouched with one hand on her hip, the other pushing at her long blonde hair, in perfect imitation of her mother. Bobby's eyes filled with tears and he stomped over to one of the sofas to pout in peace behind a potted palm. Susie stayed with her mother.

With an impatient sigh, the woman slapped her palm onto the bell on the registration desk. "Unbelievable," she muttered. She turned to see Frieda and Helen for the first time. "Can you believe this?" she complained. "The water has been turned off again. Two days in a row! I'm trying to take a shower before lunch and get the kids cleaned up, and then this!" She swelled out another elaborate sigh and began to strut around the room. She was dressed in white shorts and a white short-sleeved top that was far too skimpy for the April weather, but showed off her perfectly tanned arms and legs. Helen forced herself not to smile under the woman's scrutiny of the casual appearance offered by Frieda and herself.

The woman said petulantly, "Oh, where the hell is that man?"

She had just rung the bell again when a man appeared from the depths behind the registration desk. Helen was sure that the sleek black hair brushed back from his forehead was produced by artificial means — it was far too shiny to be real. Judging by the thick jowls and leathery skin, the man must be in his fifties. His voice boomed out over the lobby with false joviality, no more authentic than the seventies-style nugget ring that weighted down his little finger. "Yes, Mrs. McKendrick, what can I do for you?"

27

"I've just about had it with the inefficiency of this place, Benson." She folded her thin brown arms over her chest and dug her heels into the rug. Susie watched, mouth open, eyes gleaming. It was clear her mother was preparing for a lengthy session. "The water in our room has been turned off. Either you get it going again immediately, or my husband, the Senator, will hear about this when he gets back from Washington. That's Washington, D.C., by the way."

During Mrs. McKendrick's speech Benson had quietly searched for, and located, a sheet of paper. "I understand your feelings, Mrs. McKendrick, but we did notify everyone that we'd have to turn off the water for two hours today." His face remained calm as he placed the sheet before her. She leaned over, arms still folded, and read it. He continued, "You see, because of the drought the county is requesting that we do some repairs to our water system. The company we contracted with could only fit us in this morning, so we let all our guests know about it on Saturday night." He fumbled with the sheet under Mrs. McKendrick's glare. "In fact, I'm sure we put these notices up . . . Marta? Could you come out here a moment?"

A door behind the desk opened wider and a small dark woman stepped out timidly. She was thin and tired-looking, with dark circles smudged under her eyes. The pale blue shift she wore, sporting an "SW" logo on the collar, hung loose on her body. She pushed her lank black hair behind her ears. "Yes, Mr. Benson?" she asked.

A discussion ensued, in which Benson and Marta tried to reassure Mrs. McKendrick that all the guests had received timely notice of the water stoppage. Helen rose briefly from her chair to browse through a display of brochures that graced the counter. When she sat down again, armed with colorful pamphlets, she'd had a good look at the office — the huge desk that dominated the room, covered with messy stacks of paper and adorned with a gilt-framed picture of a young blonde woman. Wife, daughter? Helen concentrated on the conflict again.

Red-faced and unmollified, Mrs. McKendrick clacked across the parquet. "That notice says the water will be on after eleven-thirty. It's now eleven forty-five. I expect to be able to take my shower right now. Susie, Bobby, come on," she spat out as she left. The family's hasty retreat was blocked by the simultaneous entrance of an elderly couple clad in matching blue sweatsuits and white sun visors. A mumbled, angry, "Excuse us," and the McKendricks were gone.

"What on earth was that all about?" The woman straightened her twisted sweatshirt and scanned the room in an amazed glance that took in Helen and Frieda from their refuge near the desk. "Did you see that, Chester? She nearly ran me down."

"Don't worry about it, Louise," Chester said, patting her arm. He strode up to the desk, where Benson and Marta were talking in low tones, and proceeded to pat out a cheerful drumbeat with his hands. "Hey, you two! How's it going?"

"Fine, fine. How are you and Mrs. Palmer this morning?"

"Just dandy. We took a little walk around the lake today." He leaned closer and lowered his tone.

29

"The police took down the yellow tape earlier this morning — you know, what they put up around the rocks where that woman fell."

Benson's hearty smile flagged only for a moment. "Yes, I know. Things should get back to normal around here now. Nothing to worry about, not a thing," he boomed.

"A sad, sad thing," Chester intoned, shaking his head. In the background Louise humphed loudly. "I guess they've decided it was a suicide?"

Benson shook his head solemnly. "I'm afraid the police haven't told me anything, Mr. Palmer," he intoned at a lower, more reverent volume. "I'm sure it must have been an accident."

"Damn terrible thing," Chester Palmer said with a worried look on his face. "I guess there'll be more about it in the papers tomorrow, huh?"

"Perhaps there will. Marta, we'd better try to get the dining room opened up. Were you able to get hold of Joe, or Nancy?"

"Yes, Mr. Benson. They are already in the kitchen. I will wait on the tables." She slipped back into the office as quietly as she'd emerged.

Benson sighed and shook his head. He wiped a hand across his flushed brow. "Don't know where we'd be without Marta," he said to Chester. "She keeps us afloat — her and my little girl."

"Say, where is that pretty daughter of yours?" Chester wanted to know. He ignored the bristling of his wife as he grinned at Benson, who was picking up a sheaf of papers.

"Miranda? Oh, she's been at her sister's all weekend. I haven't seen her since Friday night."

"Yeah, I noticed she hasn't been around."

"You would," Louise muttered. "Why can't you leave that girl alone?"

Marta came back out of the office just then, and Chester turned a brilliant smile upon her.

Although Marta ignored him, this was too much for Louise. She watched the smile on her husband's face turn into a leer, then she pulled him away from the desk. "Come on, it's lunchtime," she said, marching him out of the room.

Benson sighed with relief, then noticed the quiet presence of Helen and Frieda. He turned on the bright smile again. "Anything I can do for you ladies?"

Frieda smiled back. "Not at the moment, thanks."

"You've been having a busy morning," Helen said, watching the young woman steadily.

"Oh, no more than usual. It's just this water thing — they sprang it on us by surprise. It makes things a little difficult." He beamed absently at them. "I do hope you'll go out in one of the boats today and enjoy this weather."

"I understand you had quite a bit of excitement on the weekend," Helen went on. "A woman died — or so I hear."

"Yes." His broad face clouded over, and the look Helen had glimpsed a moment ago — when he'd called to Marta for help — stole over his features. It was a look of confusion, of uncertainty. He glanced at the counter as if hoping to find help there in the bills and receipts and notices. "It looks as though it must have been an accident."

"She was staying here, I think." Helen ignored the kick to her shin from Frieda, but turned to catch her glare. She was about to press on but her

31

questions were forestalled by another dramatic entrance.

He was tall, strongly built and very masculine in faded jeans and plaid flannel shirt. Everything about him exuded ruddy male health with a woodsy overtone, from the rough curly brown hair, the sunburnt features, down to the scuffed cowboy boots. But upon close examination there were signs of wear and tear — the distended belly above the belt buckle bespoke too many beers, and his muscles swayed, flabby, beneath the clothes. His voice grated hoarsely, as though he'd just woken up.

He leaned heavily on the desk. "Any messages for me? It's O'Neill, Alex O'Neill, room fifty-two."

Benson looked glad of the interruption. Shuffling through his papers he finally admitted there were no messages.

"Nothing? You sure? All right. Wait a minute, how about for my wife, Amy O'Neill? Maybe they called for her instead."

"I'm sorry, Mr. O'Neill, there's no message."

"Damn!" He slammed one meaty paw down on the desk, then backed off when Marta flinched. "Sorry. It's just — this message is really important. Could you let me know the minute you get it?" He nodded at Benson's assurances, then stomped back out without ever glancing at Helen and Frieda.

"Come on. Let's try out this dining room we've been hearing about." Helen got up, stretched, lounged out of the room. As soon as they were safely out of earshot, she said to Frieda, "What the hell did you kick me for? That hurt!"

"I can't believe what you were doing. That man

32

was really upset about the whole thing, and you kept asking him questions."

"Hey, let's get one thing straight." She grabbed Frieda's arm, made her stop and listen. "This is not a party. We're not here to be nice to people. We're tying to find out what happened to Jill on Saturday night. If any of these people are involved, I hope I get them good and upset before I'm through."

"Well, Lord knows I'm never able to stop you. I just didn't think it would be like this."

"You'll get used to it. Anyway, I managed to get a look at his office."

"So I noticed. See anything important?"

"Yeah. The usual mess, stuff all over the desk, not enough room — and a big framed photograph on the desk. Pride of place, silver frame — the works."

Frieda shrugged. "Probably his wife."

"She looked too young. But I know one thing — it sure looked a lot like the girl I saw climbing on the rocks where Jill died."

Frieda paused at the door to the lounge. The tantalizing smell of food drifted through the door that Frieda held open, and they could hear the tinny sound of Muzak piped in. "Aren't you coming?"

"Not yet. You start without me." Helen headed across the parking lot to the trail that led to Still Waters Lake.

Chapter Five

"So this is where it happened, huh?"

The girl Helen had seen in the photograph on Benson's desk jumped up from the rocks. She stood before Helen in the flesh — golden-haired with lovely pale skin and light blue eyes. She hadn't heard Helen walking along the sand, and the noonday sun caught her poised to flee to safety, like some wild creature frightened by an intruder. The baggy sweater, which seemed to Helen to be a badge for young women these days, along with the loose cotton trousers, couldn't hide her slim figure. Long, graceful hands swept her shining hair from her face, although the wind kept tossing it back.

"Sorry, I didn't mean to startle you," Helen said, climbing up on the rocks to join her. She hoped, by means of constant chatter, to keep her there and talking. The girl faltered, not sure if she should stay or leave. Helen saw, now that she was close, the red rims around the eyes, the long dark lashes still wet with tears. Helen looked away and let her eyes travel up the distance of the rock that dropped from the highway down to the beach. "That's quite a distance," she went on, pretending not to notice the other's emotion.

"Yes," the girl whispered.

Helen continued to prowl around the rocks, stepping carefully and deliberately avoiding eye contact. "My friend and I — we're staying over at the hotel down the road. Still Waters, it's called. It wasn't till we actually got here that we made the connection. Between this woman that died and the hotel, I mean. I don't suppose —"

"What?" she asked sullenly, apparently ready to dislike Helen immediately.

"Do you know anything about it? Are you staying up at the hotel, too?"

Helen asked this question reluctantly, hating to play the part of a ghoulish curiosity-seeker. Strange for a private eye to have qualms about this sort of thing — but she always preferred cases where she could be more straight-forward, less forced to act out a role.

Her questions seemed to upset the girl even

more. The blue eyes welled up with unshed tears. She turned her face away and started moving tentative feet into footholds for climbing down.

"Hey, I'm sorry. People are always telling me I talk too much. I didn't mean to upset you. Actually, I'm only asking because I knew her slightly."

"You knew Jill?" She stopped awkwardly, with one foot on the sand.

"Back quite a number of years ago, yes, I did. I hadn't seen her in a long time, though." Helen clambered down to join her, and they stood regarding each other while Helen prattled on. "I take it she was a friend of yours? I'm really sorry. Like I said, I hadn't kept in touch. Last time I saw her she was going through some tough times. I guess she was still doing journalism, or some other kind of writing. She was staying up at the hotel, too, wasn't she?"

Helen chattered away while being examined, feeling the discomfort of those blue eyes studying her closely. Apparently she was judged to be all right — or, if not all right, harmless. The girl's face softened a bit when Helen wound up her spiel.

"Yes. I knew her too, in a manner of speaking."

"Oh, really? Then you were here the night . . . I mean . . ." Helen paused to show delicacy.

"Well, I wasn't here all weekend, but I live here. My name's Miranda Benson."

"Benson? Then you must be related to the owner, right?"

"That's my dad." Miranda smiled briefly, then started off across the sand. Helen tagged after.

"Now that you mention it, there's some resemblance. Something around the eyes." They walked slowly towards the path going back up to the hotel. Helen sighed, stretched, and said, "Look at that water! It must be great to go out and see it every morning."

Miranda glanced at her, shrugged. "I don't know. It's a little different if you have to look at it every day . . . Sorry, I guess I'm kind of depressed about what happened."

"Hey, if Jill was a friend of yours —"

"Sort of. I met her a while back. Last summer. I even suggested she might want to come up here and stay at the hotel — you know, do some swimming and boating, stuff like that . . ." Her voice trembled and shattered under the weight of emotion. "If it hadn't been for me, Jill would still be alive. I mean, she wouldn't even have come here or anything."

Even though they had met only moments ago, Helen felt an urge to put an arm around her thin shoulders, to hug her close and comfort her. Instead she stuffed her hands into her pockets and waited for Miranda to gain control. "You can't blame yourself for what happened," she finally said. "Not unless you were the person who actually pushed her off the road down onto the rocks."

Miranda turned a startled, tear-stained face to her. "But — the police said it was an accident."

"Oh, I know, I know. I'm sure they're right. I'm just trying to tell you not to feel guilty. Jill went out on that road of her own free will — it was nothing to do with you."

The sunlight broke through a cloud and bathed the beach in a golden glow. The light caught Miranda's hair, lit up her eyes, and Helen had to look away so as not to betray her physical reaction

37

to her. "Thank you," Miranda said softly. "You've made me feel better. And I don't even know your name," she finished, smiling shyly.

"Helen Black." They shook hands, and Helen had a fleeting impression of strength veiled behind a facade of feminine weakness.

Miranda frowned, crinkling her forehead. "I don't think Jill ever mentioned your name," she said, then caught herself.

Helen thought, then you were close enough to know the names of Jill's friends.

"Well, like I said, we'd lost touch over the years. And we were never all that close," Helen lied.

Miranda nodded. "A long time ago, you said."

Helen was amused at the implied accumulation of years she must have attained in Miranda's youthful eyes. Amused — and a little stung to be passed over as too old for further interest.

"Well, I bet Jill was having a good time here."

"I don't know. Maybe it wasn't quite the right setting for her." They had reached the edge of the path, but Miranda lingered on the sand, as if reluctant to go to the hotel. "Things aren't so hot around here, anyway," she said as he eyes threatened to fill with tears again.

"What do you mean?"

"I shouldn't be saying this, and my dad would kill me — no, never mind." Then the tears came again in full force. Miranda plopped down on the sand and sobbed. When she could catch her breath, she stammered out, "Everything is going wrong. Every year we have fewer and fewer people staying here. The lake is drying up with the drought. We can't get anyone but Marta to stay and work with us. And we keep on getting stupid stuff like the water being shut off, getting all the guests mad at us."

Helen, unnerved by the onslaught of weeping, kneeled down in the sand next to Miranda, unsure of her next move. She was saved from any action at all by the yelling of a woman's voice further up the path. "What the —" she started.

"Oh, God," Miranda moaned. "It's Louise Palmer."

Helen remembered Mrs. Palmer from the lobby. In a moment she saw the telltale white sun visor bobbing up and down like some strange bird peeping out from the trees. Louise Palmer still wore the blue sweatsuit, but now the ensemble was accompanied by designer sunglasses that reflected everything around her like a mirror. Helen saw her image, and that of Miranda, in a rounded fun-house parody in Mrs. Palmer's eyes.

"Oh, I thought it must be you," her voice blared out at them.

Helen watched her taking in the sight of the two women sitting together on the sand, and she wondered what was going on behind those huge silver lenses.

"I wanted to talk to you. About Saturday night?"

"Well, I've only just gotten back, Mrs. Palmer." Miranda scrambled to her feet and dusted off her clothes. Helen was impressed to see how quickly she was able to compose herself. "What can I help you with?"

Mrs. Palmer shook a finger at her. "You know I always want fresh towels at my room on Saturday nights. In fact *every* night. And I distinctly recall telling you so."

"I take it there was a problem about the towels, then?"

"That Mexican girl you have, what's her name . . ."

"Marta. Her name is Marta, Mrs. Palmer."

"I think you should speak to her, you or your father. She just isn't doing her job right."

"Certainly I'll look into it. Are you and Mr. Palmer going out on one of the boats today?" She managed to soothe the older woman into a semblance of calm. Soon they were talking about lunch, and Mrs. Palmer, having satisfied her need to complain, went huffing back off in search of her husband.

"I don't know how you did that," Helen said in genuine amazement. "The woman frankly makes me want to slap her in the face."

Miranda laughed, and Helen was caught once again by her ethereal beauty. What she must have appeared like to Jill!

Miranda said, "Oh, it's not hard, once you get the hang of it. People are so easy, usually, to figure out, and get to do things. I used to tell Jill that when she'd complain about never getting anywhere, but she wouldn't listen." As soon as she realized she'd been talking about Jill again, Miranda clammed up.

They walked slowly in silence until Helen broke the spell. "How did you meet Jill, anyway? Last summer, you said."

"Oh, just a little vacation I was on. She was — she was so different from anyone I'd ever met before. She'd traveled, been so many places, done everything —" Miranda broke off and turned her brilliant, sad smile onto Helen again. "You must think I'm crazy, going on like this."

"No, not at all."

"I hardly even know you. Maybe that's why I feel like talking to you."

"Sometimes people will talk more readily to a stranger than to someone who knows them well. Maybe they feel a stranger would be less judgmental."

They were now at the edge of the path. Across the paved driveway arched the magnificent entrance to Still Waters. Helen heard Miranda sigh.

"Well, back to the salt mines," Miranda said, with an attempt at a smile. "If my dad finds out I got here and didn't get right back to work — no telling what the consequences will be."

"See you around."

As Helen watched her wander off through the parking lot, she spied Frieda coming out of the double glass doors that led to the lobby. She waved a hand at Frieda's greeting. In a moment they were walking together back through the lobby in search of lunch.

Chapter Six

"Need a refill?"

Helen nodded, and the bartender poured a couple of fingers into the small glass. Frieda shook her head and sipped at her beer. Helen let the familiar warmth spread, welcoming the delicious sense of release. She glanced around her as she set the glass down on the spotless counter. There were only a couple of patrons besides themselves, and they were slouched into the fake leather chairs by the pool table. They stared into the distance without really seeing — devotees, she guessed, waiting for someone to show up with a cue in his hand. "Pretty quiet in here," she said to the bartender.

"Yeah, well, most people are working now." He swished a cloth over a glass with his soft beringed fingers. "Things liven up quite a bit around nine o'clock every night. We got dancing and sometimes a live band." He set the glass down, picked up another, and looked with interest at Helen. "I don't think I've seen you ladies in here before."

"No, well, we're —" Frieda glanced at Helen as if seeking an okay to go ahead — "we're staying at the hotel up the road."

"You mean Still Waters? Yeah, we get a lot of people from there coming in here for the music." He took a breath, as if gathering speed to continue, then stopped. After going for the next glass, he finally said, "I suppose you heard about what happened over there on Saturday night."

"You mean the woman who died."

"Yeah, right. The reporter. It was in all the papers, about how she fell off onto the rocks." He shook his head. "Musta been a mess when she hit ground," he said, watching them with a gleam in his eye.

"Yes, I heard. As a matter of fact, I knew her slightly," Helen said, twirling her shot glass on the bar.

"No kidding! You ain't bullshitting me, are you?" He walked over to the other end of the bar and called out to the two baseball-capped men slumped by the pool table. "Hey, come on over here! This lady here says she knew Jill Gallagher."

One of the men coughed, a heavy chest-rattling noise. "What the hell shit are you shoveling now,

43

Sidney?" he wheezed, pushing his cap back further on his shiny forehead.

"No shit, man. That chick that jumped off the cliff on Saturday night, you know?" Sidney the bartender swiveled his round face back towards Helen. "Hey, lady, I'm real sorry about your friend. She came in here a lot, you know, used to have a couple of beers before going back to the hotel."

By now the pool aficionados had ambled up to the bar and were gazing at Frieda and Helen as if the two women were exotic beasts on display. Frieda squirmed a bit on her barstool, but Helen laid a restraining hand briefly on her arm.

"Wasn't she in here the night she died, Sid?" This came from the second of the two men. He was dressed in faded jeans and a T-shirt that extolled the glories of beer. On his head was a baseball cap identical to the one owned by his companion, except that it was more encrusted with dirt. "Seems like I seen her that night."

"Yeah, she was. I remember. In fact I told the cops all about it." He reached for the bottle to refill Helen's glass. "No, no, this one's on the house," he said over her refusal. "Say, what's your name? I don't believe I caught that."

"Helen Black. This is Frieda Lawrence."

"You can call me Sid. Everybody does."

"Thanks, Sid." Frieda smiled and accepted a second beer, although the one she was working on was still half full. "So the police came to talk to you, huh?"

Sidney looked at her closely, saw that she wasn't all broken up and ready to cry over Jill Gallagher,

44

and leaned forward conspiratorially. "They sure did. I guess they figured she'd been drinking when she — when she fell."

"That's right, Sid, you tell 'em. Sorry lady, but you have to watch what ol' Sid here says." The man wheezed out a laugh, coughed, adjusted his cap once again. "He's prob'ly got the whole thing solved for the cops, don't you, Sid?"

"Hey, show a little respect!" Sid's red face turned away from them and fixed in a sullen frown. "Don't pay no attention to these guys."

"What did the police say to you, Sid?"

"Well . . ." He moved a little closer. Helen could smell his heavy cologne, the stale cigarettes on his breath. She saw with faint surprise that he was wearing some kind of makeup on his pock-marked skin, and she watched it crinkle unevenly as his mouth moved. "They think she was dead drunk when she left here."

"Was she?"

"No way!" he whispered fiercely, then stood back with a look of satisfaction. "She wasn't that drunk when she walked outa here. I know, because I wouldn't give her anything."

"Why not?"

"She didn't have any money. Not more than enough for two beers. That's all, just two beers."

Helen frowned. Frieda said, more to Helen than Sidney, "But the police must have done an autopsy and found some alcohol in her system — enough to warrant that assumption, anyway. I mean, they wouldn't just assume she was drunk without some kind of proof?"

45

Sid snorted. "The cops around this place? You gotta be kidding. They wanted it to be an accident. Less work for them."

"What do you mean, Sid?"

But he shook his head and went back to work on the glasses. "I don't mean anything. I'm just saying she wasn't drunk when she left this bar. Hell, the last thing she had was a damn cup of coffee, 'cause I wouldn't cash another check. Not when the last one bounced."

This prompted another wheeze from the man at the other end of the bar. "Yeah, Mack sure took that one out of your hide."

"Fifty bucks, and it wasn't even her own check! She said her 'friend' gave it to her."

"Bet we all know what kind of 'friend' that was."

"Well, her 'friend' sure wasn't named George or Dave or Tom or anything like that."

"No, more likely Susie or Sally, or something." Snickers and giggles sounded from the other end of the bar. Sidney's glare sent them back to their lair by the pool table.

"Don't pay any attention to those guys. They just sit around here wasting time." He scooped up some change from the bar and headed for the cash register. With one hand he dropped the change into the drawer. The other hand pulled out a flimsy piece of paper. "The poor woman is dead and all my boss can think of is his lousy fifty bucks."

Helen sat up, alert. "Would you mind if I had a look at that check, Sid?"

Suddenly his face darkened. "I don't know if I should do that. I mean, I know you were friends and all, but —"

"Hey, it might be someone else I know. Friend of a friend. If I could get hold of this person, maybe he or she could make it up."

"Well . . ." Sidney hesitated. "Just look at the name real quick. I can't let you take this." He slid the piece of paper across the bar, holding it down firmly under one finger. The black type flickered under the dim overhead lighting and Helen read the name softly to herself, then aloud.

"Amy O'Neill." She turned to glance at Frieda, who repeated the name, then stared at Helen in recognition. Yes, they'd heard that name earlier, at the hotel. The slip of paper disappeared under Sid's hand.

"That's it, now. I shouldn't of even let you see that." He looked from one to the other of the two women at the bar. "Well? You people know this woman?"

Frieda shook her head. "No, never met her." Helen could see that her eyes were bright with excitement, but she betrayed nothing as she sat sipping her beer.

"Oh, well." He ambled back to the cash register and replaced the check in the drawer. "Worth a try, I guess."

"Aside from the fact that she only had a couple of beers that night, do you remember anything else?"

Sidney considered them from the cash register. The heavy face grew more thoughtful. "Sounds like you don't believe it was an accident, either." When neither one responded, he shrugged. "Only other thing I remember is how long she stayed in the can."

"What?" Frieda asked.

"She was in the john an awful long time —
maybe a half hour. I remember 'cause a couple of
women were bitching about it. We only got the one
john here for women, and she hogged it that night."

"The bathroom." Helen felt like laughing. It was
hardly the sort of information she'd expected.
Suddenly a broad beam of sunlight entered the room,
and Helen felt the warm air from outside rush in as
someone came into the bar. It took a few moments,
in the dim lighting, to make out the garb of a
sheriff's deputy.

"What's going on, Sid?" The young man eased
himself onto a bar stool just on the other side of
Frieda, who received a bright warm smile from him.

"Hey, Jim." Sid spoke with dampened enthusiasm.
"Cup of coffee?"

"Black with sugar." He placed his sunglasses on
the bar, and Helen studied his smooth, almost
babyish features. The cherubic smile was calculated
to charm, but the blue eyes that met hers were
steely and cold, like chips of ice. "Well, we cleaned
up at the lake today. It's open for business again."

"I heard." The name tag glimmered "J. BOWLES"
as he reached for his mug.

"Yeah, Jim, Sid's been solving your little mystery
for you. Says it wasn't no accident. Ain't that right,
Sid?" The chorus by the pool table cackled.

Jim heaved a patient, exasperated sigh. "Now,
Sid, you gotta stop all this." The small hand that
held the steaming mug belied the powerful muscled
arm bulging beneath the drab shirt. "I know you
liked the woman, but that isn't any reason to keep
going on about it." He beamed at the bartender, who

turned away, blank-faced, to polish the sparkling glasses.

"Hey, Jim. Them two gals knew her — the one that died."

"Really?" Helen felt the steely eyes surveying them both. "Well, I'm really sorry about your friend. There was nothing anyone could do. A sad case." He sighed and shook his head, burdened with the responsibility of having to take care of so many careless citizens. "I sure hope old Sid here hasn't been upsetting you. He means well — just remember that."

"Oh, he hasn't upset us at all," Helen replied, rising from her stool. "We were just going. Thanks for the drink, Sid."

"Come back anytime." They walked out under Jim's stare into the sunshine.

Frieda heaved a sigh of relief. As soon as they had safely traversed the parking lot she began to laugh. "I'm sorry, but it just sounds so silly. The bathroom. Poor Jill." They strolled along the narrow wedge of grass rimming the highway. Frieda kept her face turned to the sun as if delighting in its warmth. They were within sight of the hotel's sign when Frieda stopped in her tracks.

"Helen. It's only just occurred to me."

"What?"

"You've probably been thinking about this all along. It's one thing to walk back to the hotel from the bar in broad daylight — but why on earth would Jill do that in the middle of the night? Where was her car? She had one, right?"

"Last time I talked to her, she did." Helen

watched Jim's car flash by while she answered Frieda. Did she imagine it, or had Jim been studying them as he passed? "I have been wondering about it."

"Why haven't the police found it yet?"

"Probably because they weren't looking." She resumed walking. "Let's see what we can find out about Amy O'Neill."

Chapter Seven

The first time Helen saw Amy O'Neill, the woman was administering a resounding slap to her husband's face. It was on the wooded hill behind the hotel. At first Helen had no idea who the woman was.

Frieda had gone back to their room, complaining of a headache. "I'm sure I'll be fine by dinnertime. Maybe I just need a quick nap." Helen had watched her go up the stairs, suspecting that what Frieda suffered from was a bellyful of poking her nose around, asking questions, watching Helen in action.

Back outside, in the fading afternoon light, she stood still for a moment, taking stock of her surroundings. Across the wide paved semi-circle that spread before the entrance was a signpost in Still Waters Lodge's usual fake rustic log lettering: "TO THE LAKE." Helen dutifully followed directions and found herself on a shady path.

Helen was no country girl. Her street in Jackson, Mississippi, had housed what was referred to as the poor white trash section — the only trees visible there appeared around Christmas time. Although she knew enough to tell that the so-called forest around Still Waters was mostly evergreens, Helen couldn't distinguish specific types. Her feet scrunched brown, dull needles strewn thickly along the path. Seeing these, as well as the sparse branches dotted here and there with patches of bright green, Helen realized she was walking through a tinderbox waiting to blow up. The drought was taking its toll even on these hardiest of trees.

A breeze from the lake riffled her hair. No more than a ten-minute walk down to the sand, she noted. Once or twice, on her way to the water, Helen thought she'd found another path leading off through the trees in another direction. Each time she ventured off the main trail, however, she found only dead pine cones, more dead needles, and a few frightened squirrels. Helen pulled twigs and needles from her hair and fought her way back to the main path. It was after the last of these attempts to forge a new way through the woods that she heard the sound of voices.

Helen stayed two or three yards away from the path and waited, barely breathing. She turned her head slowly, trying to judge where the voices were coming from. After a few moments she could tell that the two people speaking were also stationary. It sounded as if they were further below, closer to the lake. A man and a woman and they were arguing. At first they spoke in intense whispers, then greater emotion took over and they forgot to control their voices.

Helen examined the ground beneath her feet. She thought she could move without making too much noise if she went slowly keeping an eye out for low branches. She made her way with cautious steps, placing each foot with care. Inwardly she felt her usual flush of guilt at eavesdropping. It was probably nothing — a lover's tryst turned sour, a meaningless squabble over some petty subject. Somewhere in her mind she felt Frieda's disapproval, but she pushed it down and concentrated on movement. Soon, behind the shelter of three closely planted shrubs of indeterminate species, Helen could hear everything clearly.

The low hanging branches between Helen and the arguing couple kept their features hidden from her, but by the man's large loose build she guessed that it might be Alex O'Neill. Once she heard the voice again she was sure — it was the man she'd seen striding into the hotel lobby a few hours before. Then the woman might very well be Amy, his wife. Who else would he talk to in such an angry voice? It was likely only spouses could give rise to so much hate. Helen leaned out carefully from her hiding place to get a better look at the signer of the bounced check that was sitting at the Lame Duck Saloon. All she saw was a flash of bright red hair

53

that glimmered in the shafts of weak sunlight. Cursing the dead foliage that made silent movement impossible, Helen settled down to listen.

Alex's voice reached her first. "We're not going till I say so. Unless you want me to go to the police with what I know."

There was a shocked silence, then, "You wouldn't dare."

"Oh yeah? Just try me. If you make one little move to leave without me, you've had it, bitch."

"Jesus, Alex, what the hell is wrong with you? I'm your wife, for God's sake! Anyway, just what is it you think you're going to tell them?" Amy's voice gained in power and Helen saw the red flash again. "Are you going to march into the sheriff's office and explain how your wife was sleeping with another woman? Huh? That she was so dissatisfied with her lawfully wedded husband she went to a woman for sex?" Amy began laughing hysterically. "That's a good one, Al. Just try that out on the police."

"Goddamit, will you shut up?"

"Afraid someone will hear you, lover? You're the one who chased me down here, demanding to talk to me." Helen heard snapping sounds, as if someone were breaking the little branches. "If this is your idea of conversation, I've had more than enough. I'm going back up to the hotel."

"Oh, no, you're not."

Helen heard sounds of struggling — grunts, gasps, the flat sound of flesh hitting flesh. Then one good ringing slap that echoed through the trees. That was all Helen needed to hear. She leapt out from behind the shrubs and headed in the direction of the couple, slinging branches out of her way as she went, certain she'd see Mrs. O'Neill on the ground, being pummeled by her husband.

Instead, she saw a red-faced Alex O'Neill holding his jaw with one huge hand, the other hand raised in mid-air to ward off another blow. He didn't even notice Helen's presence. His wife was only half his size — just five feet tall, with pale skin and huge green eyes set below deep red hair that fell across her flushed forehead. Breathing hard, she turned around to see Helen approach. Helen heard her mutter, "Satisfied, Alex?"

He made an incoherent sound, raising his hand as if to strike back, then saw Helen hurrying through the bushes. The hand fell to his side.

"I thought I heard something," Helen began, watching them closely. "Everyone okay?"

Amy O'Neill spoke calmly. "We're fine. We were just going back to the hotel." Her green eyes met Helen's with a level gaze, as if daring her to say or do anything. She started off back to the main path, then stopped and looked back at her husband. "Coming, Al?" she asked sweetly.

He cleared his throat and answered hoarsely. "No, no, I'm going on down to the lake for a minute. You go on ahead." He reached out awkwardly to his wife, but she evaded his grasp and swiftly went back through the trees to the main path. Helen followed after, with one quick look at Alex. He was already hurrying away from the scene of his humiliation toward the lake, obviously glad to be away from prying female eyes.

As soon as she had reached the path and nearly overtaken Amy, Helen called out to her. Amy turned around. "Look, this is none of your business. I don't

55

need anyone's help or sympathy, all right? Just leave me alone."

"I'm not here offering help. You look like you're doing just fine on your own."

"Then what is it you want?"

Helen caught up with her in two more steps. They were alone on the trail. The sun was dropping down rapidly behind the hills that divided Berkeley from Contra Costa County. Amy's face was suddenly thrown into shadow. Helen was unable to read the other woman's expression, but as she stood there, catching her breath, she could feel the woman's anger.

Helen said, "I just wanted to let you know about the check over at the Lame Duck Saloon."

Amy's laugh conveyed puzzlement — and relief that it wasn't something worse. "What the hell are you talking about?"

"A check you made payable to Jill Gallagher. I'm afraid it bounced."

The air seemed to grow cold with a quick jolt. All the warmth of an early spring afternoon drained away. Amy's hand slid up and down her bare arms in an attempt to warm herself. She took a step closer to Helen. "What did you say?"

"Jill cashed your check at the bar down the road. It came back no good. They'd sure like to get their money back."

Amy now stood close enough so that Helen could see the fear in her face. "Just who the hell are you?"

"My name is Helen Black. I'm — I was a friend of Jill's. From way back. I think you must have been a friend of hers, too."

"And why would you say I was her friend?"

Helen smiled, turned her face so that she could look down at the water in the distance. Alex O'Neill was nowhere in sight. "I gave her money myself, once in a while. She was always in need of something or other. And she was very convincing, wouldn't you say?"

"Helen Black, Helen Black. Not the kid from Mississippi?"

"That's me." Helen turned back to look at Amy. She wasn't expecting a welcoming embrace from Amy at this news, but she wasn't sure how to interpret the blank stare coming from those green eyes. What had Jill said about her?

"You used to be a cop, right? And now you're a private eye."

"That's me."

Amy raised her hands in mock surprise. "Don't tell me — you're out here investigating a case. Wouldn't by any chance be that you're snooping around to find out something about the dear departed?" She spoke with bitterness, but her voice trembled.

"Well, I'd just sort of like to know what happened. Wouldn't you?"

"I can tell you exactly what happened." Amy stuck an arm out in the direction of the highway, nearly hitting Helen with her gesture. "The stupid bitch got drunk, stumbled out along the road, and fell down and broke her neck. And that's all, no matter what anyone else says."

Helen nodded, looking out in the direction where Amy pointed. "Mmm. Are you sure?"

"Of course I'm sure. So if you'll excuse me —"

"She left a message on my answering machine minutes before she died," Helen called after Amy, who was climbing up the path rapidly. "She said she was being followed. And that she was scared."

Amy stopped and turned her face up to the sky, sighing in exasperation. "Like I said, she was drunk. If you knew her like I did —"

"Just how well did you know her, Mrs. O'Neill?"

"Who the fuck made you God? It's none of your damn business. Jesus, that's all I need, another dyke in my life."

"Then I'll just have to draw my own conclusions about you."

"That's right. You think whatever you like, Ms. Private Eye. Just leave me out of it."

Helen followed close behind. The woods were almost completely dark now, the path covered in shadows. Up ahead they could see the hotel lights shining over the asphalt of the drive. "I'm going to find out what happened, with or without your help, Mrs. O'Neill. But I would like to know anything you can tell me about Jill. You were obviously close. I hadn't seen her for some time myself. If you were her friend —"

"Look." Amy stopped in her tracks at the entrance to the path. "As far as I'm concerned the bitch can rot in hell. Does that answer your question?"

Helen watched her go into the hotel, then followed at a distance. Yes, she thought to herself, it does answer my question. Either you really did hate her — or you once loved her very much. Remembering the scene she'd witnessed in the woods, Helen thought she knew the truth.

Chapter Eight

"You can be sure I'll tell everyone I know to stay the hell away from your hotel from now on," Sunny McKendrick shouted at Mr. Benson. "And believe me, the Senator and I know an awful lot of people we might have encouraged to come here." With that she flounced out of the lobby, her body tightly corseted in stiff jeans and tank top, wobbling slightly on high-heeled boots. One heel caught on the edge of the floral carpet, nearly causing her to stumble and fall.

Mr. Benson turned his head away to avoid seeing

such a satisfying sight. God, what a day. He leaned back against the registration counter, drained of all energy but relieved beyond words that the lobby was finally empty of people.

He let out a heavy sigh and walked down the narrow corridor that led past the small office to the private rooms where he and Miranda spent what little spare time they had. He could hear her moving around in her room. Her door was slightly ajar, releasing a thin shaft of light into the hall. Without a warning knock, he pushed the door open and looked into the room.

His daughter sprang up from where she'd been curled at the foot of her cot. Miranda's shaking hands slammed the cheap spiral notebook shut, trapping loose papers inside its covers. Benson couldn't see her expression in the shadows as she shrank back from him on the bed.

He sighed as he sat down on the cot. Its old springs squeaked out in protest at his weight. "How you doing, punkin?" he asked. "You look beat."

"I'm fine, Daddy. How are you?" She stayed huddled at the foot of the cot but still within his reach.

"Well, we've seen better days, haven't we, sweetheart?" He forced a chuckle out. "Between the drought and Mrs. McKendrick and the people that are staying away in droves, I've just about had it."

"You say that every year, Daddy."

"And every year it's true. What's that you're working on?" he said, reaching out for her notebook.

"Nothing, Daddy." He was too quick for her brief gesture of concealment and a moment later he was flipping through the loose pages, stopping briefly now and then to read. Finally he closed the notebook. "Then you were sleeping with that bitch," he said quietly. Miranda tried to dart out of his reach, but his huge hand collided with her cheek in a swift slap. Tears welled up in her eyes, but she was silent. "If only your mother were still alive, she'd know what to do with you. Our own daughter, our little girl, turned into a sick pervert." With a disgusted shake of his head, he got up and left the room abruptly. The cot heaved under Miranda's stifled sobs as he slammed the door shut.

Once she had herself under control again, Miranda picked up the notebook from the floor where Benson had tossed it. She checked it to see that all her notes and papers were intact, then slid it under the thin mattress. She undressed with the light still on, then lay, stiff, beneath the sheets. One hand found stray threads on the sheet near her chin. Staring at the ceiling with eyes frosted over with pain and anger, her fingers tore and shredded, enlarging the rip that had already begun.

"Put that bottle down. You've already finished your performance for the night." Amy O'Neill yanked the bourbon away from her husband, spilling some on the carpet as she did so. He made no protest, no move to stop her. He regarded her with amusement from the floor where he'd crashed a moment ago. His huge body, once muscular and powerful, sagged with the flabbiness of age and lack of use. Amy stood over him and looked down with disgust as he shook with silent laughter.

"Go ahead, step all over me. I love it." He rolled around until he was sitting up. "It's my profession now. Since I gave up teaching." Amy made an attempt to walk away but Alex grabbed her leg, clasping it around the ankle. "Didn't think I could move so fast anymore, did you?"

"You make me want to vomit."

His hand began caressing her, running slowly up her calf almost to the knee. "A bird's eye view," he said softly. "Now I see what Jill was so hot about."

"Let go of me, you bastard," Amy hissed through clenched teeth.

"Whatsa matter, can't you spread 'em for your own husband?" With a wry chuckle he let her go. "Never mind. What's the point?"

"Don't put it all on me. You haven't been able to get it up for years now. Besides, you knew about me when you asked me to marry you." She carried the bottle into the bathroom, and a moment later the gurgle of liquor sounded hollowly throughout the room.

"Yes, my love, I did indeed," he answered as she came back out of the bathroom.

"Then why are you still here with me?" Amy demanded as she tossed the empty bottle into the trash with a dull clink.

"Because I still love you. And somewhere underneath all that anger, I think you still love me. It's just that you loved Jill, too."

They stayed silent for a few minutes, Alex breathing heavily, Amy perched tensely on the edge of an easy chair. Finally she said, "So what are we going to do about it?"

Alex managed, after a severe effort, to heave

himself up to a standing position. "Nothing. I think it's already been done, don't you?"

"Am I supposed to understand that?"

"You should. I'm saying that part of our little problem has been solved, out on the shore of that cute little lake." Alex looked around him aimlessly. "Now where the hell did I put that bag?" he muttered.

"You can't possibly be talking about Jill," Amy said, her green eyes frozen on her husband.

"Ah, here it is." He unzipped the small case and with a big smile pulled out a bottle of gin. "Never overlook the shaving kit, darling."

"*You*, accusing me of murder? That's a laugh. If anyone had a motive it was you, Alex."

"Me? I never accuse anyone. I just let the facts speak for themselves. Anyway, an obstacle to our marital bliss has been removed, no?" He took a deep swallow, throwing his head back. "Want some?"

"Go to hell." Amy switched off the lights. Alex started to laugh hysterically, standing there in the dark. She snarled, "Will you shut the fuck up?"

"It's just so funny. You tell me to go, and I'm trying to tell you we're already there. Like that play by Sartre — there's no exit. No way out," and he kept laughing.

"Come on, Louise, we've had enough excitement for one day." Chester sat up in bed, exposing his bright orange silk pajamas to the harsh glare of the bedside lamp. "Get away from that window, now."

"I swear, you never like to do anything," Louise

grumbled. She padded over to the bed, adjusting her hairnet. "I just think I might get a glimpse of the Mexican girl again. I told you I saw her last night with that guy wearing a ponytail —"

"Yes, the whole place knows about it now."

"Well, I only told those queers about it. You act like I blab all over the place."

"Now, Louise, you gotta stop talking that way. They're people, just like you and me."

"Huh!" She watched Chester's orange-clad back as she rolled over to get back to sleep. "Well, for your information, I refuse to be put in the same category as queers," she said, reaching for her cold cream. She continued to look in the direction of the window as she slathered on a white muck and started to work it into her skin. "Besides that, the woman they found out there was queer, too."

Chester gave up. He sighed and sat his scrawny frame up in the bed. "Now how the heck do you know that, Louise?"

"Never mind. You said I talk too much." With a prim gesture she screwed the lid back onto the cold cream and lay down, placing her hands across her chest in a quasi-religious pose.

"Louise, you'd better tell me. You know you will sooner or later."

"Well, I just so happened to see a certain young lady out by the water a few days ago kissing that woman. Right on the mouth, too. I almost threw right up out there in the woods." She shuddered pleasurably at the memory. "Disgusting, I say."

"So disgusting you stayed and watched the whole thing, I suppose?"

She threw him a look and went on. "For your

information I did not. I went right back to the hotel. I was going to tell you about it, but you were having your nap. Then I thought I should wait and see what happened before I talked about it." Worry creased her white-coated features. "I wonder . . . I wonder what she was doing the night it happened."

But Chester was already snoring. With a sigh of irritation, Louise switched off the light and continued to stare into the dark.

Outside the night was cold, but the room where the young woman lay was stifling. Her entire body tensed when the steps sounded in the corridor. A rectangle of light grew into the room as the man opened the door and stepped inside; then it disappeared into blackness as the door closed once again. She could smell the stale sweat as he took off his uniform, carefully removing his nameplate, badge and holster in a stylized ritual reminiscent of holy procedures. The steely eyes that had earlier studied Helen and Frieda now looked down on the girl who lay naked and trembling on his bed.

"*Hola, Marta. Como estas?*" he breathed as he lay beside her. "Now, now, *chica*, just take it easy. I ain't gonna hurt you — not much, anyway." He clapped a hand over her mouth when she began to cry. "Remember what we talked about before? How this is just a little deal we got worked out? You play your cards right, and everything will be fine, just fine." He grunted as he moved on top of her, pushing her small body into the position that pleased him most. The sound of her quiet sobs faded in his ears as he pried her shaking legs open and entered her. "Fine, fine, fine," he mumbled, shoving in quick rhythm. Minutes later when it was over, he slapped her — just one swift movement that brought blood to her lips. "I told you to stop that, didn't I?" She turned on her side and put her fist to her mouth to try to keep quiet.

Chapter Nine

Helen shifted uncomfortably in the booth at the
Lame Duck Saloon. The hamburger she'd just
devoured at the hotel had been fried in too much
grease for far too short a time. Leaning back on the
red vinyl with a sigh, Helen surveyed the bar. It
presented a much livelier face to the world now that
the sun had gone down. The band was warming up
and the barstools were almost all taken. Helen
winced with each tinny twang of steel guitar. She'd
spent most of her adult years trying to forget the

country music her parents had listened to by the hour.

Frieda suddenly appeared, each hand holding a tall drink. "What is it?" Her wide dark eyes studied Helen's face with concern. "Aren't you feeling well?"

Helen grimaced, then forced her expression into a grin. "I think it's that hamburger. I'm not sure they completely killed the poor cow."

Frieda shook her head, chuckling. "I told you to have a salad, like I did. You know how your stomach reacts to grease."

"Well, when in Rome. This will make it all better." Helen took a deep swallow. Frieda craned her neck to see what she'd been writing. "A couple of lists," Helen said as she slid the paper over the table. Frieda squinted at it in the dim red light of the bar:

Chester Palmer
Louise Palmer
Alex O'Neill
Amy O'Neill
Mrs. McKendrick
Bobby McKendrick
Susan McKendrick
Senator/Congressman McKendrick
Roger Benson

"A list of suspects?" Frieda asked as she handed back the sheet of paper.

"Not exactly," Helen yelled as the band played a rendition of "The Orange Blossom Special." Helen cleared her throat and made another effort to make herself heard. "Just the names of people at the hotel over the weekend."

"You don't seriously think the McKendricks had anything to do with this, do you?"

"Not really. I'm just making things clearer in my own mind. Remember how on the phone message Jill talked about getting out of that hotel as fast as she could? Well, one reason for that might have been someone staying there. Someone following her, watching what she was doing."

Frieda nodded. She waited for a break in the music, then, as the crowd applauded, asked, "You said lists, in the plural. What else have you got there?"

"Just this." The microphones whined while Frieda read out the words.

accident — car
accident — fall due to drunkenness
murder — argument that got nasty (on the
    side of a highway??)
murder — followed and pushed off road by
    someone

"Yes, yes, I know, the last two sound crazy." The MC announced a medley of Hank Williams hits, and the band obeyed with verve. Helen leaned closer to Frieda, pushing the small candle in red glass out of her way. Frieda followed suit, and Helen caught the scent of her freshly washed hair, clean and sweet, piercing through the stale smell of the bar. Frieda frowned down at the papers, unaware of the reaction she was provoking across the table. Finally Frieda looked up and shook her head.

"The biggest question, of course, is why? Why would anyone want to kill an old —" Frieda stopped herself in time, and even in the awful red glow Helen could tell she was blushing in shame.

"It's okay, Frieda. You can say it. Jill was a washed-out loser. An old good-for-nothing reporter with nothing left to say. She drank too much, got on everyone's nerves, and generally made herself a pain in the ass. I know." For the first time since she had been alone with her thoughts of Jill in the kitchen of her house at Berkeley, Helen felt a wave of emotion threaten to take over. She glanced, unseeing, around the crowded room to gain enough time to get hold of herself. Finally she said, "But I can't believe this was an accident. Not after that phone call."

Frieda looked down, fiddled with the candle, then her drink. "What about Jill's car?" she asked. "Any news on that?"

Helen shook her head. "No, nothing."

"Did you call your ex-partner about it?"

"Yeah, he's checking on it. He says he'll try to call back tonight. If anyone can weasel information from another cop, it's Manny. But I'll bet whatever you like that they haven't found it."

"Hey, how you gals doin'?" Helen turned around to see who was breathing so heavily into her neck. Just behind her a short, wiry man with a huge nose and arms covered with thick blond hair leaned over the back of the booth, his hands tapping merrily on the seat. Each word was punctuated by the smell of cheap beer. "Y'all havin' a good time tonight?"

"Lovely, thanks." Helen turned around pointedly but her pursuer was not about to give up so easily.

"Why'nt you let me buy you a beer? Me and Bo —" He indicated a pale faced man, whose chest peeked through the strained buttons of his shirt — "we thought you two lovely ladies might like a little comp'ny."

"Yeah," Bo joined in. His grin revealed a lack of teeth. Helen turned around again and caught Frieda's eye.

"We were just getting ready to leave," Helen said loudly. "Thanks anyway, guys." Frieda was already standing up and gathering shoulder bags for their departure. Bo, however, was much faster. Before Frieda could edge her way out of the booth he settled his bulk next to her, still wearing the same toothless smile.

"Now, that ain't very friendly, is it? All we want is just to share a coupla beers with you ladies."

Helen's suitor hadn't yet taken his place next to her. Instead he leaned over closer. "I think we's all goin' to be real good friends, ain't we?"

Helen watched, fascinated, as Frieda relaxed and turned on a huge smile. With one hand she reached for the beer Bo was offering. "Of course we are, boys." Deftly she turned the bottle, aiming the foaming stream directly at Bo's crotch. His widened eyes and slack mouth announced that she hadn't missed. "Just as soon as you get cleaned up," she said sweetly.

Bo crawled out of the booth, both his hands covering his soaked crotch. Helen took advantage of Frieda's surprise attack to vacate her seat at the same time. As they made their way through the crowd that surged and parted around them, Helen heard the screech, "You goddam fucking bitches!" By then they had fought a path to the narrow hallway that held two public phones and the restrooms.

"God, if it's like this on a Monday night, I'd hate to see it on the weekend," Frieda said as they dodged a woman darting out of the ladies' room. A tall thin man wearing a cowboy hat squeezed past and grabbed one of the telephones, only to start cursing when he saw the torn yellow scrap of paper that read OUT OF ORDER in block letters. On the other phone a young woman, barely twenty-one, was in the midst of an argument over someone named Bill, who was a lying cheating no-good sonofabitch. Helen stood still as if mesmerized.

"Helen? Helen, what's wrong? Come on, let's get out of here." Frieda moved in front of Helen. "For God's sake, what's the matter with you?"

"That's the women's bathroom."

"No shit? What a discovery. Look, Helen, two assholes are out there, one with a very wet crotch, who'd probably like to make things a little uncomfortable for us, you know? I think we'd better get out of here before Bo figures out where we are."

Helen suddenly smiled. People shoved by her but she took no notice. "That was a pretty good trick you pulled on Bo."

"Yeah, well, I don't know about that, but let's just get out of here." Frieda looked anxiously over her shoulder, then froze. "Great. Here they come."

Without word or warning, Helen grabbed her arm and pulled her closer. She leaned one shoulder into the door of the restroom and shoved. Fortunately the bathroom was deserted. In another moment, they were inside, the door closed and locked behind them. Frieda watched the bolt slide into place with a sigh of relief. "Great idea, Helen. One of your best. I had no idea detective work was so exciting — just imagine, only a few days ago I was sitting around bored in my studio. Now I get to hide from a pair of shitheads in a bathroom in the Lame Duck Saloon."

"Take it easy." Helen was walking around the room with small careful steps, studying the walls.

"I don't know what the hell they put in that drink you just had, but it must have been some pretty good shit," Frieda said, staring at her lover in amazement. "When do you start walking on the ceiling?"

"Would you calm down?" Helen had finished with the cracked plaster on the walls. Now she was studying the floor. The grimy linoleum stretched a bare yard in front of the sink, then another couple of feet in front of the single toilet. Helen ran her hands over each gritted crevice, her face close to the floor. When a horrible thump sounded on the door, Frieda gave a soft yelp. "I think someone wants to come in," she whispered.

"Wait." Helen listened with her, then turned back to the floor when the thumping stopped. "Probably just someone fighting to get to the phone."

"Do you mind telling your faithful assistant what the hell is going on?" Frieda hissed, crouching beside her.

"I just realized something," Helen said, sitting back on her heels. "Remember how Sidney said she spent so long in the bathroom? And the message on the telephone — Jill said she'd just hidden her evidence where no one would ever think to look for it."

"Yeah, so?"

"I think she put something in here." Helen said, "Just wait, Frieda," when she saw her rolling her eyes. "Sidney said she went to the bar — went right in here — stayed for nearly half an hour. Then she goes out and makes a call to me, telling me she's got proof and that she's hidden it just a minute ago."

Frieda sighed. "Well, since we're in here I guess it's worth a try — until someone has to take a leak." She stood up. "I think I'll work on the walls."

Helen paid no attention. She was looking closely at the bare pipes exposed on the wall above the toilet. Frieda moved over to the watery mirror and gingerly ran her fingers around the edges. It hung loosely on the wall, and her hands dislodged flakes of yellow paint into the rusted sink. A few flakes took up residence under her nails, some of them sharp enough to cause pain. She jerked her hand away with a muttered curse. The sudden motion edged the mirror down from its already precarious position and scraped an extra inch of paint into shavings that floated to the floor. Frieda looked up, certain that the mirror would crash down into a million shards, but after a couple of tremors, it stayed on the wall. Frieda breathed a sigh of relief, shaking her head. Then she saw it.

"Helen."

"Hmm."

"Helen, get away from the john and come over here."

Dusting her hands on her jeans, Helen stepped over to the sink. She followed Frieda's gaze up the wall to where a slim edge of paper peeled over the top of the mirror. With careful hands Helen pulled gently at the paper.

"What is it?" Frieda asked.

"Bingo," Helen said. It was long — a sheet taken from a legal pad. Helen held it up under the bare bulb that lit the bathroom in a sickly yellow glare. "I'm not sure what this is, but that's definitely Jill's writing." Quickly she rolled the paper into a neat scroll. "Come on, let's take this back to the hotel."

Chapter Ten

"It seems kind of silly to drive the car for thirty seconds to get back to the hotel," Frieda was saying as she and Helen breathed deeply of the fresh air outside the Lame Duck Saloon. "It's not that late, anyway. Only around nine o'clock."

"Are you forgetting what happened out here on Saturday night? I'm not taking any chances, and neither are you."

"Evenin', girls."

Out of nowhere, Bo and his crony appeared, illuminated by one of the towering streetlamps erected at strategic points over the parked cars. His crotch was still damp, stained with a dark patch that had spread halfway down his legs. He reeked of alcohol. He was no longer smiling as he flexed his simian forearms against his burly chest. He nodded towards his friend, who leaned with seeming nonchalance against a dirty red pickup, circa the late fifties, that lurked in the gloom a few yards away.

"Dave and me, we figured maybe you didn't understand us before." When Bo grinned, his gums displayed a few cracked and stained teeth. In the fluorescent light of the lamp, his sweaty face gleamed with unnatural warmth. "We was just tryin' to show you two very lovely ladies a good time, seein' as how you're not from around here."

"Yeah, right," Dave grinned, the first utterance he'd made all evening.

"There's certain sports, for example, we like to play at in the nighttime," Bo went on, walking closer. Dave followed not far behind. While Bo spoke, Helen was gauging the distance back to the saloon, as well as the sprint she'd have to make to get to the car, while pulling Frieda along with her.

"Helen —" Frieda started in a frightened undertone.

"Go get in the car," Helen snapped, putting her keys firmly in Frieda's hand.

"But, Helen —" She stood her ground, paralyzed, uncertain what to do next.

"I said get in the car!" Helen hissed through clenched teeth. "I can handle this."

Without a word, Frieda began to hurry off, but her path was blocked by Dave, who moved easily around the parked cars that stood in her path. He waited, his grin turning into a leer, directly in front of Helen's car. "Hey, Bo!" he called out. "I got me one, right over here!"

"Good for you, Dave," Helen said. She kept looking at the door of the bar, willing someone to come out, while she walked slowly in Frieda's direction. One glance told her that the service station across the road was deserted, just as it had been on Saturday night. Except for the noise escaping from the bar they might have been the last four people remaining on the planet. One or two cars sped by on the highway, their drivers intent on following the road. The strip where they stood in an uneasy circle was shielded from view by rows of cars. Helen had no doubt that their persistent suitors were well on the way to drunken oblivion — too tanked, perhaps, to fully realize what they were doing — but their sheer physical size, and the fact that there were two of them, might be enough to defeat any notion she had for self-defense. At best, she might be able to engage them both in attacking herself, while Frieda ran back to the bar for help.

Frieda seemed to read her thought, for she was backing away from Helen's car and working her way through the rows to the door of the bar. Dave was following, but his balance was impaired just enough so that she was able to keep a bit of distance between them — the space of two cars at least.

A knife flashed in the dull light as Helen made a move to close the distance between herself and Dave. Bo's knife. Frieda hadn't seen it. She kept moving, starting to run as she broke free of the line of cars and made for the door.

"Motherfucking bitch!" Dave yelled after her. In

his fury he stumbled against a small sports car, bent over and howled in surprise and pain.

"Quit your cryin', asshole," Bo breathed. "We still got us one." He moved up to Helen with more swiftness than she could have thought possible, and she felt the smooth coolness of the blade on her arm. "Let's just get moving now, sweetheart," Bo muttered, his hot breath grazing her neck. "We got to hurry up, so your little friend don't find us."

Dave, apparently expert in his teamwork with Bo, had limped back to the truck, and Helen heard the engine roar to life. Once they were all inside, with Helen pressed up close between them on the front seat, the door of the bar opened as a yellow square in the darkness. Helen made a sudden struggle to free herself from Bo's grasp, then felt the sharp edge of the knife pricking her neck.

Bo shoved her down, her head forced against his knees, and placed a hand on her head. "You just keep quiet now," he said.

Helen fought down the urge to fight back — there was no chance with the two of them pressed so close against her. She could feel Bo's heavy hand weighing on her neck. Surely Frieda must be in the bar by now, raising the alarm. Any moment now help would be on the way. She looked around her, hoping to see an opening for struggling free.

But their truck was already grinding along the curve of the entrance way. In another two seconds they would be out on the highway, headed for God knew what forsaken part of the surrounding woods. Helen briefly cursed herself, not for the first time, for stubbornly refusing to get a gun. She hadn't wanted to use a weapon in her new career, hoping to break the stereotype of hardboiled private eye — and her years on the police force had given her an unshakable hatred for handguns.

All these thoughts flashed through her mind in a matter of seconds. Then her chain of reason mixed with fear broke, as she saw, unbelievably, a circle of alternating blue and red light through the grimy windshield of the pickup. The crackling static of a dispatcher's monotone sparked through the air, uttering its code of numbers and letters. Helen slid out from under Bo's weakening hold on her body as the pickup slowed to a stop. With an almost sickening sense of relief she realized that the cavalry had arrived. She didn't even care that it was the hard-edged Officer Bowles she'd run across earlier in the bar.

"Hey, boys," Bowles said, slapping one hand down on the hood of the truck. The dirt rose up under his palm and floated down on his freckled hand. He'd shed his sunglasses, but the metallic blue eyes had the same cold stare Helen had seen that afternoon. "What's happening tonight?"

"Nothing," Bo answered, sullen. He leaned back and let Helen climb over him. "We was just giving her a lift home," he finished lamely, jerking his head at Helen, who now stood on solid ground.

"Is that so?" Bowles said. He sauntered along the side of the truck until he reached the passenger side, where Bo leaned out the open window. "Now, what's this I see?" His hand flew out, and before Bo could stop him he held up the small knife in his outstretched palm. Bo said nothing, merely folded his arms and looked away.

"I think I'll keep this as a little souvenir. I don't

suppose you'd like to come along with me and explain where you found this?" He swiveled his round face to Helen. "Maybe you'd like to come along and say a thing or two about what went on here this evening?"

Helen looked at Dave and Bo, slumped down in their seats. "They shouldn't be driving around in their condition."

Bowles sniffed the air around Bo's head. "Shit, boy, what'd you do? Take a bath in it tonight?" He looked at Helen again, his eyes expressionless. "Sure you don't want to press any charges?"

Helen shook her head. "Just make sure these men get tested for alcohol level, that's all."

She made a move to get away, but Bowles blocked her. "I believe we met before. This afternoon," he said, peering into her face.

"That's right."

"You're the friend of that reporter, right? I didn't catch your name?"

"Helen Black."

"Staying up at the hotel, right?"

"Yes." The scrutiny was making her very uncomfortable. Suddenly she felt just as vulnerable as she had two minutes ago, when crammed in the pickup between Dave and Bo.

He kept staring at her, then shifted his feet, his body relaxing, as if he'd come to a decision. "I may need to look you up tomorrow morning to talk about these two goons," he said, sliding a notebook out from his shirt pocket. "How long will you be at the hotel?"

"I'm not sure. Two more days, maybe." She watched him make a note. For the first time Helen

81

had a sense of what it felt like to be on the other side of the uniform and badge — the strain of talking and moving normally, even when there was nothing to be guilty about, the forbidding sight of the pen moving across the paper, the knowledge that one's name would show up in a report on someone's desk in the morning.

With a final nod and stare, Bowles let her go. Helen walked slowly back up to the car, hardly seeing Frieda's joyful face.

"My God, Helen! Are you okay?" Frieda took her by the hand and led her to the car. Helen saw Sidney, the helpful bartender, flanked by a couple of anonymous patrons eager to get in on the fun. First a death, now a near abduction and rape — too good to miss.

"I'm fine. The fun's over, guys," Helen said, managing a weak smile. She let Frieda bundle her into the car and they squeezed past the pickup and Bowles' patrol car, then turned out quickly onto the highway.

"Jesus, I've never been so scared in my life," Frieda said, near tears. "Are you sure you're okay? They didn't hurt you?" she pressed, steering with one hand and taking Helen's hand with the other.

"I'm all right. Nothing happened. The guys in white hats showed up right on cue." Her answers came short and clipped. Helen was astonished to realize that her predominant emotion was neither fear nor relief. It was anger — anger and humiliation at having to be rescued in the first place, like some goddam damsel in distress from a third-rate romance novel.

"God, I can't wait to get into our room and get

in bed," Frieda sighed as they pulled into the parking lot of Still Waters hotel.

"Not me." Helen got out of the car before the engine was off.

"What? What did you just say?"

"I'm not ready for bed. There's work to do."

Chapter Eleven

"You can't be serious."

"Oh yes I am." Helen stood, half dressed, in front of the bed in their hotel room. She dug through the small heap of clothes she had just pulled from her suitcase. Jeans, T-shirts, even a bathing suit packed in the hope of warm weather, tumbled across the shiny blue bedspread. Frieda sat cross-legged on the other single bed. Her hand, holding a hairbrush, stopped in mid-air as she watched Helen select a thick sweater from the pile. "Look at that paper again."

"I've already looked."

"Don't you see it?" Instead of pulling on her boots, Helen sat next to Frieda, holding the yellow sheet they'd found in the bathroom at the bar. "These lines — it's some kind of map." Frieda sighed, watched Helen's fingers trace the drawings. "This is the hotel, and this is the saloon."

"And the numbers?"

"Ten and twelve, followed by p.m. It means something is happening at those hours. Something Jill thought was important." Helen tugged the sweater over her shoulders and was looking for a matching pair of socks. "What this represents is the highway, the stretch of road between the bar and the hotel. And this —" She drew her forefinger along the thin black line leading away from the unevenly drawn box that stood for the Lame Duck Saloon, "this must be some path that goes back to the hotel through the woods." Helen retrieved her boots from under her bed. "What time is it?"

"Almost ten."

"That gives me a little time to take a look at this place."

"Good God, Helen! I cannot believe you are going off on some wild goose chase in the middle of the night on the basis of a child's treasure map." Frieda bounced off the bed, tossed her hair from her eyes and flung the brush down on the bedspread. Arms folded tight, she stood over Helen, coldly observing her struggle with the boots. "Why are you so sure Jill left that there, anyway? Maybe someone else did."

"That's her writing, all right." Helen glanced down at the sheet again and read the words aloud.

"Shed. San Pablo Dam Road. Photographs. Priest."
The boots were finally on and she stood up. "It
means something, Frieda."

"It's pathetic. Even if she did leave this in the
bathroom, it all adds up to nothing. To see you
running around like a fool —" Frieda broke off, sat
down again slowly. "Helen, what's really going on?
Why are you doing this?"

"We've only gone over this a million times,
Frieda. I think she was telling the truth when she
said someone was following her. Just because nobody
else believes it, doesn't mean it wasn't true."

"But to go running out there, in the middle of
the night! Helen!" Frieda took Helen's hand in her
own. "You don't feel guilty about Jill, do you?"

Helen stopped cold. She sat very still but refused
to look up from her boots. "Why do you say that?"
she asked quickly.

"Because you're not approaching this the same
way you do normally. Most of the time you look at a
case logically, not taking a bunch of stupid risks."

"There's no risk here, Frieda." Helen stood up
abruptly and picked up her flashlight. "I'm following
a lead. Are you coming or not?"

In the silence she turned to face Frieda. "Why
are you looking at me that way?"

"Helen, what happened to Jill was not your fault.
Don't punish yourself for it."

"I'm not punishing myself. I'm just trying to
figure out what the hell happened out there the
night she died. You don't have to help me. I can do
this alone." Helen checked her pockets one more
time — the key to the room was still there. She

picked up the crude map and folded it into a small square.

"Fine. Go off into the woods, play macho hero again." Frieda picked up her brush and pulled it through her hair with short furious strokes. Helen was out the door before she finished the sentence. By the time Helen had reached the road Frieda had shed a couple of tears, found a jacket and followed her down the stairs.

Unaware that Frieda was not far behind, Helen skirted the road and with her flashlight looked for the path. Half of her felt ashamed. Of course Frieda was right, at least to a certain extent. She began to feel foolish — stumbling with a girl scout flashlight through the trees, getting her face and hands scratched and more than likely covering herself with poison ivy, as well as frightening the birds sleeping up in the branches. Even worse was the memory of the pity on Frieda's face. Helen had hoped, in spite of her own better judgment, that going to Still Waters would be a good idea — would bring them closer together, make Frieda more accepting of the career Helen had chosen. Instead, here they were, at each other's throats again their first night at the hotel.

Brooding like this while thrashing through unfamiliar foliage, Helen nearly missed the path. The sudden absence of shrubbery caused her to stumble. Her flashlight played over an expanse of dirt sparsely dotted with some indeterminate kind of weed. No more than five feet wide, the gently sloping trail led down into the darkness of the woods.

Helen played her flashlight across the path, hesitating. She concluded, as she watched the light dissipating into shadows, that Frieda was absolutely right. This was ridiculous. Should she turn back? As she rubbed her arms in an attempt to warm herself, Helen felt the folded sheet of paper crinkling in her shirt pocket. She was out here. She might as well finish what she'd started. Holding the flashlight carefully to light her way, she started moving down the path.

Now it sloped sharply downward. Helen nearly missed her footing, sliding close to the bushes toward her right. Stones skittered out before her. She steadied herself by clutching a thick branch projecting from a stubby tree, but in the process nearly lost her flashlight. Once she had caught her breath, Helen started again, stepping more slowly. The only sound she heard except for her own footsteps was the scratching of leaves and branches in the brief bursts of cold wind. She walked for what felt like miles into the woods, cursing herself for her pigheadedness.

"Frieda was right," she muttered as a leafy branch slapped her across one cheek. "I'm behaving like a child. Serves me right for running off, playing Robin Hood. Just who do I think I am —"

Suddenly there it was. Nestled in a small clearing, the shack loomed up in the thin gleam of the flashlight. Its startling presence in the gloom made it appear large, sinister. If there was paint remaining on the rotting boards, Helen could not tell its color. About the size of a large tool shed, the shack had a low flat roof and a small window on either side. For all its decrepitude, Helen realized that the windows were tightly shut, the door neatly fitted to keep intruders out — or secrets safely hidden inside. As she tried the handle, Helen knew it was too much to hope that the door was unlocked.

Well, it was worth a look in the windows, at least. The building was low enough so that she didn't have to stretch and strain to see inside. The flashlight picked out a strange shape in the center of the room. It took several moments for Helen to realize that she was looking at an elaborate setup for a camera. There was a tripod, an assortment of lenses on a table, boxes that Helen guessed contained rolls of film. But what the hell was all this stuff doing out here in the middle of nowhere? A corner of the room looked as though it had been set up as a miniature darkroom. The circle of light picked out the dull sheen of a steel sink tucked behind a thick dark curtain.

Helen made her way around the side of the shed toward the back, hugging the wall as she went. Maybe there was another way in through the other window. Just as she reached the other side of the building, she heard above the rustling of the trees the low hum of voices. Helen moved back behind the shed, crouched low, and kept her breathing light and noiseless.

"You're sure no one saw you?" It was a man's voice, a deep hoarse whisper.

"Yes, yes, I am sure." There was something familiar in the tones of the woman who answered him, something faintly foreign in the cadence. "We have to come here, make certain everything is gone." A rattling metallic noise told Helen they were opening the door to the shed. A moment later white light shone through the window just above her head. Helen crouched in further, hunched in shadow.

"There were some photographs left. Yes, here they are."

"What about all this equipment? We shouldn't leave it here." He spoke above a whisper now, but his voice was filled with fear. "I'd better take it back with me."

"Yes, you take it. I have no place to put it." The woman sighed. "It was time we moved this part of the plan anyway. We have been working here too long."

"Help me carry this."

Helen didn't dare lift her head to watch them leave, but the noise they made with the equipment would cover any sound she made while following them. The light went off as suddenly as it had come on, and as soon as she heard the door being locked, Helen crept around the edge of the building. Hardly daring to breathe, she peered around the corner and saw two people struggling with the tripod and boxes of film. If they hadn't been so earnest, it would have been comical — the tall, rangy man and his petite companion. Helen waited, letting them gain a little distance. The man's flashlight wove a wild pattern in the trees; on one of its orbits the beam reflected off a long flat surface. Helen nearly cried out in recognition when she realized it was Jill's beat-up Volkswagen at the edge of the clearing.

Seeing the pair up ahead struggling with the equipment, Helen decided to take a brief detour and check out the car. She wrapped one end of her sweater around her fingers in case of prints, and checked the door. It was firmly locked. Then, hiding the glow with her body, she risked a quick flash of light into the interior, reassured that the other visitors to the forest were too occupied to notice. A brief glimpse told her nothing — beyond the fact that Jill's car was kept in the same state as her apartment.

It was easy to catch up to the couple on the path. Helen stayed at a safe distance until she heard the sound of car doors opening and closing. She found a convenient patch of shrubbery, prayed it wasn't something that would make her itch the next day, and watched them. The vehicle was a white van at least ten years old. Listening to the engine, Helen decided it had seen better days. It chuffed out a white spume of exhaust that sent its acrid stench through the trees to her lungs. The tiny bulb over the rear license plate told her what she needed to know. Then the van was gone in a noxious puff of gas, heading down the highway towards Berkeley.

Chapter Twelve

"Shit! Take it easy with that thing."

"Sorry — I know it hurts, but we've got to get that cut cleaned out." Frieda gingerly daubed at the cut on Helen's hand with a cotton ball. A bottle of hydrogen peroxide stood open on the night table. "Thank goodness I had some bandages in the car."

"I think the patient is going to live," Helen murmured, waving the damaged hand. "I wonder what I ran into that cut me like this. I sure didn't feel it while I was out there."

"It looks pretty clean now." Frieda screwed the

cap back onto the bottle of peroxide and peered closely at the cut. "I won't bandage it yet — let the air get to it." She lay down on the bed and sighed. "Good thing those two didn't see you out there."

Helen shrugged. "They seemed pretty harmless. Kind of nervous. I don't think they had guns, but I couldn't tell in the dark." Helen laughed when she saw Frieda's face, adding, "Just kidding!"

"It isn't funny! We're not playing cowboys and Indians," Frieda said, fighting back a smile. "Actually, you deserve to be scratched up. Running off like that! You didn't even wait for me."

"You mean you came after me?"

Frieda shrugged and turned over on her side. With one arm she propped herself up on the bed and regarded Helen. "I started out, but I didn't get very far. By the time I reached the road I decided it would just make you mad to have me tagging along, like your kid sister or something."

Helen lay down on her side, facing Frieda, holding her hand out carefully in front of her. "I'm sorry I lost it back there. I guess you hit a nerve. I do feel guilty about Jill. I should have done more, tried to take care of her better." She stopped when she saw Frieda shaking her head.

"You're not responsible for the entire world, Helen. Jill had to live her own life, make her own choices."

"I know. It's just that — well, if I'd taken more time to visit her, help her out — the way she helped me." Helen relaxed onto her back, closed her eyes and let Frieda's gentle touch work on the tension in her muscles. "She helped me feel more comfortable with myself. I was this awkward, naive mess when I first moved in with Aunt Josephine. I hated myself for the way I loved women. I couldn't stand who I was. Jill made everything seem all right, like it wasn't the end of the world just because I was different."

"Thank goodness for that," Frieda breathed into Helen's neck. "I guess I owe Jill quite a lot." Helen lay very still, feeling the weight of Frieda's body and its softness and warmth against her own. But a nagging thought persisted. Her eyes flew open.

"Frieda."

"Hmm?"

"I have to do something. I have to let the police know about Jill's car."

"Oh." Frieda sat up. "I guess you do, huh? Right now?"

"Well — I have an idea. Manny is working nights. I could give him a call now and ask him to pass the information along."

"Why not wait until the morning and call the Contra Costa County police?"

"They're bound to ask me what the hell I was doing out there in the middle of the night. It could be a little bit awkward. Besides, Manny might be able to check out the license number on the van for me without causing too much suspicion."

"Sounds logical. Tell you what — I'm going to take a shower while you call him."

She bounced off the bed, shedding clothes as she went. The hot water was going full blast by the time Helen got her ex-partner on the phone.

"Where the hell are you, Watson?" he boomed at her.

"I'm at Still Waters Lodge."

"Why does that sound so familiar to me?" he groaned.

"It's a hotel on the border between Berkeley and Orinda. Just inside the county line. Sort of a combination of Town and Country meeting Howard Johnson's on the hinterlands of John Birch country."

"Doesn't sound like you. Wait a minute — I got it. The one who fell off a cliff or something, by the lake."

"That's the one." Helen's hand hurt much less now. She moved her fingers around, wincing as she started to pull off her jeans.

"Why do I get the feeling there's a connection between that and your own presence there?"

"Never doubt hunches. I have a little bit of information to pass along." She told him why she was calling. "Could you sort of make that known to your buddies out here?"

He snorted. "Buddies? Shit, these mothers like to pretend they live on another planet from the loonies in Berkeley. Do you know they still call it Berserkeley? I thought that went out with hula hoops." He sighed deeply in exaggerated, mock travail at her demand. "I'll see what I can do. Yet again do I put my stellar career on the line for a drinking buddy."

"I'm touched. And now I'm going to ask you to risk yourself a little bit more. Could you check out a license number for me?"

Helen hung up after hearing Manny promise to try to get back to her in the morning with any information he could dig up. She managed to pull the rest of her clothes off with the use of one hand, then looked aimlessly around for the promised

95

bandage. "Frieda?" she called out, heading for the bathroom. "Where did you put the bandage?"

The bathroom was enveloped in steam. Cool air displaced the mist when Helen opened the door. Frieda's body was shown in vague outline on the frosted glass of the shower door. Helen watched the soap bubble and froth on her dark skin, dissolving under the rhythmic, circular motions of her hands. The water swirled out from her head as she flung her hair from her eyes and arched her back to rinse the soap from the dark loose strands. With each upward movement of her arms, her breasts lifted, gleaming in the water. Helen no longer felt pain in her hand when she opened the shower door and slipped inside.

"How about some company?"

"I thought you'd never ask." Frieda moved away from the stream of water, allowing Helen to stand under the shower head. "Is your hand okay? Does that cut hurt?"

"What cut?"

Frieda worked the soap into a thick lather while Helen stood still under her hands. She lingered on her breasts, kneading, massaging warmth into them. One hand slipped between her legs and repeated the slow, smooth motion. Helen felt a moan well up in the back of her throat.

"Not yet. Not here. There's not enough room," Frieda said between brief, soft kisses. They quickly toweled each other dry and went to one of the single beds. Frieda climbed on top of Helen, lying so that their breasts met. Her tongue, hot and slick, felt its way around Helen's mouth, tasting and touching.

"God, it's been a long time," she murmured as her mouth traveled across Helen's back.

"Too long," Helen agreed. Her own hands circled Frieda's small waist to position her so that her hips rested above Helen's thighs. Without thought, without words, their bodies sought the most satisfying motion, surging and yielding against each other in steady beat. The curly dark hair between Frieda's legs teased at Helen's own. Their heat and moisture mingled. Just as Helen was beginning to lose herself in the pleasurable tension building in her groin, Frieda moved away. An involuntary moan escaped Helen, but Frieda immediately stopped the sound with a kiss.

"Not so fast, honey," she whispered, and suddenly Frieda's mouth was licking and sucking a path down her chest, across her belly, finding its destination between Helen's legs. Her fingers gently parted the tender lips and slid deep inside. Helen shuddered and moved in response to the probing fingers, crying out almost as soon as Frieda's tongue laved the swollen flesh. Before her body had stopped trembling with the final waves of her climax, Frieda lifted herself up and ground her hips into the soft, warm sweetness between Helen's outstretched legs. Her back arched as she said her lover's name in a soft cry. Helen felt herself coming again at the sensation of Frieda's smaller vulva rubbing against her own. This orgasm was longer, more intense than the first. It ended with both of them collapsed, sweating, in each other's arms. Finally Frieda moved away to switch off the lamp on the night table.

Helen stared at the ceiling. Even in the dark she

could feel Frieda's eyes studying her. "Feeling better?" Frieda asked.

"Yep." Helen impulsively reached out one arm and hugged Frieda close. She started to giggle.

"What?" Frieda asked.

"I'm just wondering what room service would make of this sight."

Frieda snuggled close, pulling the covers up over both of them. "We could always say it got too cold in here," she said drowsily, almost asleep.

Helen could never fall asleep after making love with the swiftness that Frieda did. It was as if the sex act performed some kind of magical release for her lover, while for Helen there was always some part of her that kept cool and distant, watching the whole thing from afar. Helen knew that Frieda must be aware of this, but chose not to comment on it. Still, as long as she saw to it that Frieda was satisfied, what did it matter?

Helen sighed, closed her eyes, willed sleep to come. Of course, because commanded, rest eluded her. Instead a panorama of the events of the day floated across her mind. In spite of the tensions, the bad moments, the arguments that had threatened, but not quite developed into full-fledged fights, Helen thought that she'd managed to keep things pretty much under control. As if to emphasize the ease with which everything was falling neatly into place, Frieda murmured in her sleep and nestled into Helen's shoulder.

Helen kissed her hair absently and began to map out the next day's activities. First she'd talk to Manny — get the rundown on what was going on with the van. Then she'd do what she could to talk to the O'Neills again. After that she might run by Jill's apartment. Helen had no idea whether or not Jill had any family — she'd never talked about anyone. Maybe she could find a way to get into the apartment, take a look around. There might be a clue as to what Jill was working on when she died.

When Jill died — the realization of Jill's death came crashing down on her in the darkness. With a shock that made her feel ill, she discovered that the memory of Jill's features was already fading from her memory. She tried to bring the familiar face back to her mind, but it remained fuzzy, soft-edged, tantalizing her as if mocking her efforts. It was then that Helen knew — this was about herself, not about Jill. Frieda had spoken the truth all along. The fake heroics, cloak-and-dagger skulking in the middle of the night, were more to prove something to herself than to honor Jill Gallagher.

Her complacency shaken, Helen finally tumbled into an uneasy sleep, troubled by odds and ends of strange dreams.

She woke to blazing sunlight and the shrill bell of the telephone. She eased Frieda off her shoulder and groped for the receiver. Her voice grated a coarse hello.

It was Manny. "Rise and shine, Watson!"

"What time is it?" Helen mumbled, squinting her eyes against the sun.

"It's nine o'clock, sleeping beauty. Time for good little girls to get up — but of course you don't fall into that category."

"Spit it out. What have you got?"

99

"I've been busy all night. I got the word out about your friend's car. The sheriff will be checking it out this morning."

"What about the van?" Helen felt Frieda stir and then crawl out from under the covers, heading for the bathroom.

"Well — I traced the number for you."

"Yeah? And?"

"You're not going to believe this."

Chapter Thirteen

"The van belongs to a priest?" Frieda stopped rubbing her hair dry long enough to stare at Helen in amazement. "What on earth is a priest doing out there with a woman? Stealing stuff for the poor box?"

"I know, it doesn't make any sense. But that's what Manny said." Helen flopped back down on the bed and closed her eyes. "None of this makes any sense. But it has to. I just have to figure it out." She opened her eyes to see Frieda combing her hair. The spray of water from the wet strands misted over

Helen's face. "Manny told me the address on the van's registration. St. Bonaventure's, over on Martin Luther King Drive."

"That's where that soup kitchen is, right?"

"Yeah. In fact, I think it's run by the church."

"Well, it doesn't seem likely that a priest who's dishing out food to the homeless would be throwing women to their deaths." Seeing the expression on Helen's face, she muttered, "Sorry. That was thoughtless."

Helen sat up, shrugged. "It's okay. It's true. I have no idea what the connection might be. But there must be something." She rolled lazily off the bed and started looking for her sneakers. "Want to come along?" she asked hopefully.

Frieda shook her head. "I don't think so. Someone has to stay here on the homefront and slog it out, hotshot, while you go off to win medals."

"What do you mean?"

Frieda leaned over Helen, bringing her face close. "I mean, maybe I would be a lot more useful out of your hair for a while. Why don't I find out what I can from the other people staying here? Then I can report back to you at headquarters, chief." She saluted, snapping her heels.

Helen had to laugh in spite of herself. "And how do you propose to worm information out of them?"

"Ah, you forget the importance of the arts." Frieda picked up a small sketch pad from the bottom of the bed. "I thought I'd sit outside at some strategic point and corner my victims with my amazing skill at portraiture. Not bad for a novice spy, eh?"

"You're wasting your talents. CIA material."

Frieda leaned down again to receive a quick kiss that developed into a lingering embrace. Helen felt faint stirrings of lust, that stayed with her as Frieda backed away with a happy smile.

"More of the same later," she tossed over her shoulder as she headed for the door.

"Promise?"

"Promise."

"Wait!" Helen grabbed a sweater off the back of a chair near the bed. "You'll be cold sitting outside today. Take this."

"Thanks." Frieda turned to go, hesitated, then sat down on the bed with Helen. "Just one thing. Don't worry, it's not a lecture — just a thought."

"Shoot." Even as she answered, Helen felt her stomach muscles tighten with dread.

Frieda spoke slowly, obviously choosing her words. "You said just now that you couldn't see the connections between all these people, all these events. The O'Neills, Jill staying here, the drawing we found, the shack out in the woods. Right?"

"Right."

"Well — I just hope you're ready to accept it, if there isn't a connection between them. I mean, between these things and Jill's death. You were a cop, Helen — surely you, of all people, know that a lot of times things just happen. They just are. Life is like that. The way Jill died — well, it really might have been a terrible accident."

"I know. Somehow I felt doubts last night, for the first time since she died." Helen reached to stroke Frieda's cheek. It was a tender gesture, a gentle touching. The surprise in Frieda's face made Helen feel ashamed. "I guess I'm not a lot of fun to be around, am I? I'm not really there for you in the way that you need. I don't know why you stick around."

Frieda moved away to cover her own emotion with a shaky laugh. "You certainly keep me from being bored." Her hands twisted the fabric of the sweater Helen had tossed at her.

Helen watched her steadily. "Why do you stay, Frieda? God knows you could have any woman you wanted. Why me?"

"It's not that I haven't thought about that, tried to come up with an answer myself. Maybe it's because we're so different, you and I. You like to believe life is logical — that things are connected in mathematical patterns. All you have to do is see that pattern, and you can figure out your life, make plans, predict the future." She turned bright eyes and a sad smile to Helen. "And I'm convinced that the world works in a very different way."

"You mean everything is just one big guessing game. No rhyme or reason. Go with the flow — something like that?" Helen tried to keep the sarcasm from her voice but she knew an edge of irony had crept in.

"Not exactly," Frieda sighed. "Just that maybe the patterns aren't all that clear. Nor should they be. People aren't computer programs, you know — you can't change a line of logic, turn on a switch and expect them to act the way you think they will." She got up from the bed for the second time. "Listen to me — I promised you no lecture, didn't I?" One more quick kiss and she was heading out the door.

Helen tugged at her shoelaces and struggled with her thoughts. If Frieda was right, then she'd behaved like a robot for a long time. Helen stared at her reflection in the mirror, frowning. She saw short brown hair, cut close to the scalp, dark expressionless eyes set deep above the short nose. Bunched in her jacket, Helen looked heavier, stockier, than usual. Plain Jane, she thought. A memory pulled at her, and she stood still trying to pin it down. Another time she'd worn this jacket, and felt the same confusions about her own emotions.

Then it hit her. Jill's apartment. In October. The last time she'd seen Jill alive. Helen recalled her thoughts of the night before wondering if Jill had any family, anyone who would be notified. The apartment building was on Sixth Street, near University — just a few blocks past San Pablo Dam Road. Maybe she could stop there before going on to St. Bonaventure's, talk to the super, find out if anyone else had been there. Worth a shot, anyway. Since Jill had met death here, miles away from her home, and since the police were treating it as accidental, it was unlikely they'd have bothered going through Jill's apartment or sealing it off. Perhaps a relative, one whom Helen knew nothing about, had already cleaned the place out.

As these thoughts ran through her mind, Helen searched for a sweater. She was sure the weather on the other side of the tunnels would be chilly. Then she remembered — Frieda was wearing it. No big deal. Instead she opted to wear the jacket.

Minutes later she had backed the car onto the highway and pointed it towards Berkeley. She'd briefly looked for Frieda but hadn't seen her in the lobby or around the front of the hotel. Good thing she had taken the sweater — raindrops were pelting the windshield in a slow pavane as soon as Helen reached the entrance to the Caldecott Tunnels. Traffic was light, since it was well past the early morning rush hour. Her watch read ten-thirty when she emerged from the brief dark silence of the tunnel into the gray mist of Alameda County. She easily traversed the freeway for the Highway 13 offramp that would take her down Ashby Avenue to San Pablo Dam Road, which cut a straight line west across the city of Berkeley, directly to the Bay. Helen was grateful that she didn't have to go near the University. Ashby remained relatively clear, but the side streets that led to the campus were packed with people, bicycles and cars, all slipping around on the oil-slick streets. Except for frequent stops the drive down Ashby was uneventful.

Sixth Street was just as she'd remembered it, an older section of town — the crumbling perimeter just fresh enough to be quaint rather than seedy, although well enough on the way to dilapidation to discourage buyers. Helen saw quite a handful of For Sale signs dotting the weedy lawns with red, white and blue. The light rain had released from the asphalt of the street that peculiarly California odor of oil, hot tires, and exhaust that had been pounded into the pavement by years of automotive torture. It assailed Helen as soon as she stepped out of the car. She buzzed for the manager but there was no response. Shit, she thought, she might have to wait out here for quite a while.

After a quick glance to make sure the street was deserted, Helen tried the door. Her luck was in as the latch was jammed. She stepped inside and stood quietly, but could detect no sound or movement. Her sneakers squished on stained linoleum until she reached the carpeted stairs.

Jill's apartment was on the second story, near the end of the hall. Helen realized with a start that she'd never been here during daylight hours. Jill had always made their meetings late at night, perhaps to heighten her own sense of melodrama. One more indication of paranoia? Helen shoved that thought aside as she picked her way across the carpet, avoiding the worst of the unrecognizable stains. Even the walls looked greasy, and an odor of cooking fat filled the air. Helen had a sudden flashback to her own hovel in the slums of Jackson, Mississippi — poor white trash country. The rancid smell made her want to run, retching, back out into the rain.

She'd gotten this far, though. Reining in her feelings, she was almost at Jill's door when she saw that it was ajar. Sounds emerged from the apartment. Someone was moving around in there. She could hear papers being rustled, heavier thumps that could mean furniture being moved, cabinets and doors opening and closing. Helen stood perfectly still in the hallway for perhaps three or four minutes, unsure of what to do next. It might very well be a relative of Jill's, going through personal effects with a view to removal. If so, Helen definitely wanted to speak to him or her. It might be the building superintendent, intent on getting things ready for a new tenant. Maybe even the police, though that seemed unlikely. A friend, perhaps?

In any case, it couldn't hurt to stick her head in the door, feign surprise, bluff about her knowledge of Jill's death. As she had so often in the last couple of years, Helen felt a sweeping desire for the old days, when she could go to a residence, warrant in hand and gun safely tucked away in her clothing. It made her wince to be forced to play along with these petty subterfuges. Fixing an innocent smile on her features, Helen took the extra two steps to the door and slowly pushed it open.

"Hello? Anybody home?" she sang out, hoping she sounded friendly and cheerful. There was a brief thud, as if something heavy had been dropped onto the floor. Then silence. Helen repeated her call. "Hello? It's just me," she said, hoping that she'd be taken for a visiting friend.

Still no noise, no motion. Helen walked further into the apartment, every muscle tensed for flight if it became necessary. This was bad, very bad. She began to back out of the room with every intention of flying down the hallway. Before she could act on that impulse, a figure darted past her. Helen grabbed at an arm and managed to catch hold before the intruder was able to slip out the door. Reflexes from the old days took over, and she applied far more pressure than she intended.

The person cried out and whipped around, cringing from the source of pain. Stunned, Helen relaxed her grip without letting go completely. There was no need for such force — the attempt to wriggle to freedom was weak.

Helen reached for the soft black ski cap and pulled it off. A cascade of bright red hair tumbled down and she looked into the face of Amy O'Neill.

Chapter Fourteen

Helen busied herself in the kitchen while Amy
O'Neill nursed her sorrows on the living room sofa.
After a few minutes of tearful protestations and
surly threats, the woman had collapsed into
exhausted sobs. She seemed willing to talk to
sympathetic ears, so Helen decided to take full
advantage of an opportunity that probably wouldn't
come her way again. She had no idea how much of
Amy's change of heart was due to grief and how
much to fear at being caught trespassing, but right
now that didn't matter.

Helen saw with dismay that Jill's cupboard contained only instant coffee and no tea, but she grimly prepared two cups and started a saucepan of water boiling. There was no milk, no sugar — they'd have to take it black. Except for the snuffling noises on the other side of the door, the building might have been deserted. Silence permeated the apartment, and Helen thought briefly of how Jill's body had slowly cooled on the shore of Still Waters Lake. With a shudder she took the water off the burner.

Amy took the offered cup from her and drank the coffee down as though it were tap water, gulping and gasping like a kid having a hyperventilation attack. The muddy liquid effectively stopped her tears and she wiped her wet cheeks with one shaking palm. "Is there anything to eat?" she asked in a low voice.

Helen stared at her in surprise. The woman was thinking of food right now? She thought back to the kitchen — a couple of cans of tuna fish in the cupboard, an opened container of fruit cocktail and a stale loaf of bread in the refrigerator, the remains of a pastrami sandwich on the counter next to the sink. "No, there's nothing to eat."

"Well, I haven't had a thing all day — I've been so worried." Fresh sobs threatened. Helen gave Amy her own cup of coffee and watched her slurp it up greedily.

"What are you doing here?" Helen asked quietly.

"I don't have to answer that. In fact, I could ask you the same thing." Amy pushed her hair back behind her shoulders and stared at Helen with angry, swollen eyes.

Helen smiled. "Fair enough. How about if I start?" Amy didn't respond. Helen got up from the coffee table where she'd been perched and walked aimlessly around the room, talking in a conversational tone. "I was here for the same reason you are — trying to find something. Anything that could tell me more about Jill."

Amy laughed with a ragged hoarse sound. "I thought you two were such good friends. She said you'd known each other for years, that you and she —" She broke off, looking down at her shaking hands.

"She and I what?"

"Oh, come on, it's no secret to me that you were lovers. Hell, she got in bed with every woman she could. Big deal."

"Is that what she said to you?" Helen stopped walking and sat down on the other end of the sofa. "It isn't true. Nothing like that ever happened."

"So I'm just supposed to believe you were friends? Is that it?"

"That's all it was, Amy." Helen somehow found it easy to call her by her first name. She looked frightened and helpless, huddled on the dirty sofa cushions. "We first met when I came to stay with my aunt in San Francisco —"

"Spare me the details," she snarled. The helpless look faded, replaced with an ugly pout. "I've heard it all before. From Jill."

"Do you mind telling me how you got in here?"

She shrugged and got off the sofa, setting the plastic cup down on the stained coffee table, contributing yet another ring to the collection already there. "Why not?" She reached into a pocket

111

of her jeans and held out a flat shiny object. "I had a key. I've had it for years. Whenever Alex went out of town on business I used to come over here and spend the night. Sometimes a whole weekend." She looked at Helen with a mixture of pride and contempt.

Helen shook her head. "When did your husband find out?"

Amy laughed again. "He knew all along. I guess you're thinking about that lovely scene of domestic bliss you witnessed out in the woods by the hotel. That should have told you everything you need to know."

Helen moved to stand next to Amy, tempted to slap the smug smile off her white face. Without thinking she grabbed the smaller woman with both hands, feeling satisfaction at the fear that sprang up in Amy's green eyes. Helen said roughly, "What are you doing here? What are you looking for?"

"Please —" Amy whimpered.

Helen saw her own hands grip the thin arms tighter, felt her own anger surge, then die down. Disgusted with herself, she dropped her grip and turned away.

Amy's voice trembled as she answered, "I was just looking for my things. I had some clothes, some stuff, I didn't want anyone else to find them. The police —"

"The police aren't going to bother with this place," Helen answered in a gruff voice. "They think it was an accident. They don't care what Jill had here."

"But someone else might find it." Amy was crouching by a cardboard box Helen hadn't noticed before. It was lying on the floor next to the coffee table. Something was spilling over the top and dragging on the floor — Helen guessed it was a sweatshirt. Beneath it a photo album peeked out, jammed with loose pictures and postcards that threatened to fall out of the box. A stuffed toy of indeterminate shape stared back into her face with its black button eyes.

Amy's face was shielded by her red hair as she attempted to arrange the contents of the box more neatly. "We were going away, you know. This time Jill meant it, I'm sure she did. That's why I went to that hotel. She said she would finish up this story and then she'd get back into journalism in a really big way. Otherwise I never would have set foot in the damned place."

Amy stood up, holding the box. It collapsed between her hands, her treasure spreading out at her feet. "Fuck!" she hissed.

Helen kneeled next to her and helped her gather the things. She was ashamed of having frightened her, but at least Amy was talking. To encourage her to continue, Helen said, "What was this story? Did she talk to you about it?"

"I don't know what the hell it was. Something she got started on when she went to Central America last summer."

"Do you know where in Central America? Anything at all about it?" Helen took Amy by the shoulders, more gently this time. "Talk to me, Amy. I just want to know why she died."

Amy turned a tear-stained face to Helen. For the first time Helen noticed the faint red rings of the woman's nostrils, the thin traces of blood that still streaked the skin near her upper lip. The wild eyes, the strange, erratic behavior — it all added up. Helen sighed and sat down on the floor. "Rusty pipes, huh? How many lines?"

"None of your fucking business, bitch. Do you think you're still some kind of cop or something? I don't have to talk to you."

"No, you don't." Helen leaned back against the coffee table and watched Amy as she stood up, holding the box against her chest. "I can already see everything I need to know."

"Yeah? Like what?"

"I think you loved her."

"Maybe I did. But it's none of your business."

"I loved her too, you know. Not the way you think," Helen said to her retreating back.

Amy stopped near the door, turned around slowly, took a few steps back into the room. "Look, for what it's worth — I honestly don't know what the story was about. Do you really think it was all that important?"

"Yes, I do. I'm convinced it's why she died." Almost convinced, she amended to herself.

"All she would say to me was that it was big. Really big. She was talking about going to one of the really big papers with it, or maybe *Time* or *Newsweek* magazine."

"And it was something to do with Central America?"

"I'm not sure. I just remember she started talking about it as soon as she got back. She was down there for about three months. Maybe it was El Salvador, maybe some other country. All I know is she disappeared, then turned up again."

Amy dragged a hand across her nose which had started to bleed a little. Helen looked down at the carpet, forcing her mind to focus. Amy went on, "I tried to get her to tell me what she'd been up to, but she just laughed and said I would have an autographed copy of the article when it appeared." Amy laughed bitterly. "At first I thought she must have gone off with you."

"No, it wasn't me, Amy." Helen glanced at the woman and asked the next question carefully. "Are you sure she was with someone? Maybe she went alone."

"No, there was someone else along for the ride." Amy walked over to the fireplace and glared an empty, dusty eye into the desolate room. "See this?" She grasped a small pottery vase, which seemed vaguely familiar to Helen.

With an odd rush of emotion Helen recognized it as the same vase she'd nearly broken the last time she was here — the one Jill claimed had sentimental value to her. "She said she got this down there. You know Jill — never a postcard, never a souvenir. Said they'd weigh her down. So someone else gave her this thing."

"Maybe not this time. Maybe she did get it herself. How do you know different?" Helen protested, though she knew that Amy must be right.

"Just the way she answered me when I asked her about it. She got a little nervous, and I knew. I knew everything about her, all the tricks and lies, and I still loved her." The tears were flowing down Amy's cheeks again, though Helen doubted she was even aware of them.

Suddenly Amy knocked the vase off the

mantelpiece. It bumped over to the parquet of the hearth, where it cracked and shattered into three or four very neat pieces. "There. All broke, Mommy. All gone. Just like Jill."

Helen silently watched her go. The building dove back into silence. Helen resisted the urge to pick up the shards of the vase and, after allowing Amy O'Neill a few minutes for a graceful exit, followed her path to the door. She stopped when she felt something strange under her feet. It was a photograph, probably dropped from the box Amy had been carrying. Helen picked it up. Nothing unusual, nothing out of the way. Jill herself was in the center of the picture, showing a smiling face to the camera, on her head a huge floppy hat. One hand held the hat down, the other was lifted in laughing protest to the camera, as if begging the photographer to refrain from taking the picture. In the background was a lean-to, shaded from the sun. Helen peered closer and finally was able to make out the shapes of fruits and vegetables arrayed on plain wooden planks. A heavy, dark-skinned woman looked on the charming scene impassively from behind the counter of the makeshift produce stand. A man, tall and thin in khaki shorts and with very sunburnt skin, bent over the vegetables with a critical eye. The only other person in the photograph was at the very edge of the picture, showing only an arm, a leg, and a small portion of the head. Judging by what she could see, including the length of blonde hair that floated into the way of the camera, it was a woman, although Helen couldn't decide from Jill's posture and gestures whether this person belonged with Jill, or not.

Helen turned the photograph over. *El Salvador, July* was printed on the reverse. "Fuck," Helen muttered as she jammed the photograph into her shoulder bag. "What the hell is going on here, Jill? And why did you have to call me that night?"

She could answer the last question herself: Because you were the only one left to call. Jill always ended up leaning on you in the end. And you let her.

After one last look around the room, Helen kept on toward the door. There was someone else she had to see, right away.

Chapter Fifteen

The cup of coffee on the restaurant's formica table steamed its rich fragrance into the air while Helen stared out the window. Here, on the west side of the Caldecott Tunnels, the late spring weather was still in the winter doldrums. For several more weeks fog would mist the Berkeley hills, and each morning would be a struggle to fight off the night's chill. Helen circled her hands around the mug and looked into its contents as intently as if some long-sought answer were there waiting to be dredged up. All the events of the previous night seemed very far away here, as distant as the warm sun that bathed the brown rolling hills of Contra Costa County.

"If I said you had a great body, would you hold it against me?" The voice nearly made her jump from the booth. She watched her former partner slide into the seat opposite with a mixture of irritation and relief.

"Manny, why the hell do you have to be such an asshole? Can't you just say hi, how are you, like a normal person?"

"Ah, that would blow my cover. How do you think I make so many busts, if it weren't for the fact that I have to be a total idiot to get away with anything in this town?" He grinned at her, obviously pleased to see her. His movie-star good looks — the gleaming white smile, rugged dark features, and carefully maintained body — turned several female heads. As always, he was well aware of the mild sensation he was causing among the few representatives of the student body assembled at the counter of the diner.

Manny placed his arms across the back of the booth, smiling expansively. "See, all the other guys in narcotics spend their time jerking off in the men's room while I actually go out and get some work done, keeping my pants zipped up."

"Great. You're a credit to your gender. Want some lunch?"

"Here?" He looked around him at the nearly empty room. It was modeled in garish late-fifties style, complete with miniature jukeboxes on the tables featuring Chuck Berry and Elvis. The walls were covered with air-brushed portrayals of carhops, their firm buttocks peeking out seductively from beneath tight red shorts. Kiddie-sized Thunderbirds were grouped on a display shelf near the cash register. "Well, I don't know — I mean, lately I'm really kind of into tofu and sprouts and shit like that, you know, wood chips and so on."

"Oh, right. I forgot. The gourmet cop. Next thing you'll be writing a damn cookbook. Vending machines I have known."

"And the women who love them." He flagged down the nearest mowhawk-topped waitress and promptly ordered hamburger and fries. Helen shook her head at the young woman's inquiry.

When they were alone again she said, "I'm afraid I don't really have a lot of time. I have an awful lot to do this afternoon, and Frieda will be waiting for me back at the hotel."

"Which translates into you not telling her what you're up to, is that it?"

"Not exactly. She knows I'm here in town. Come on, give."

He set his Coke down and pulled a notepad from inside his jacket. "As always, Watson, this meeting never took place," he intoned, flipping through the pages.

"I promise not to reveal your secrets under torture. Now talk," she said.

He shrugged. "Hard to know where to begin. Last summer, I guess. That's when her name first turned up in narcotics. Jill Gallagher was picked up in Calexico just this side of the border. Apparently the patrol out there was pulling some strong-arm shit — you know, scaring the poor sons of bitches trying to sneak into the country, twisting arms, that kind of thing. Your usual fascist pig behavior, as I'm constantly being reminded."

"What the hell does that have to do with Jill?"

"Hold on, I'm just getting to the good part. They found the usual stash of marijuana on the people they picked up, plus a healthy dose of crack this time. Jill got rounded up with some guys who were hiding out at the residence of a local, a —" He turned a page, squinted — "a Juan Garcia. This Juan has a small-time drug-running operation down there, promises to protect the illegals from the law if —"

"If they spend a little time helping him out."

"Exactly. It's the American way, after all. Anyway, for some reason no one could fathom, Jill was in the house during the latest raid. At first —" He stopped, took a drink from his Coke, and looked at her. "This next part isn't too pretty, Helen."

"Go on. At first, what?"

He sighed. "The border patrol figured she was crazy. Screaming about plots, the CIA, the FBI after her — all that kind of paranoid shit. When they got hold of her ID, saw who she was, they took her over to San Diego —"

"All the way over there? Oh, I get it — standard observation."

"Right. When they couldn't find traces of drugs in her body, and she still kept on about being hunted down, they figured she was certifiable." He glanced up at her, decided to continue. "So over in San Diego they kept her in restraints for the usual twenty-four hours —"

"Jesus," Helen breathed. "Sorry. Go ahead." She shut out the image of Jill straining against the thick leather straps, the tiny cell with the barred window and the metal cot, the sounds of others under observation as they screamed at their fate, the rattle of keys and buzz of electronic locks when the hall doors closed. She tried to pay attention to Manny's words.

"She calmed down pretty quick. They kept her for seventy-two hours, then the judge let her go. Usual thing — no room in the jails, no care facility that could take her. And no prior record of mental disturbances." He closed the notebook with an abrupt slapping noise, then reached for his half-finished hamburger. "Now, you tell."

"Tell what?"

"Why you need to know all this stuff." He finished his lunch while Helen related the series of events, starting with the odd phone message, the discovery of the drawing, the weird equipment in the shed in the woods.

"Photography stuff?"

"Yeah, cameras, tripods, lenses. Things like that. And that little building was damn secure. Closed up tight as a drum, new locks on the door."

"Hmm. Interesting." He nodded as he swabbed at the pool of ketchup on his plate with the final french fry.

"What's interesting?"

"Well — something else turned up when they picked up these illegals. Our friends in blue down there — or brown, or whatever it is they wear — anyway, there've been a number of refugees from places like El Salvador in Calexico. They can't ever get much information out of them. I guess when you've been tortured by experts a bit of badgering

122

from Officer Friendly doesn't seem like much. But we've been trying to figure out what happens with the ones that get through — that make it across the border and up into the States. There must be something like an underground railroad there."

"The shed." Helen sat silently and Manny watched her putting it together. She looked up, the light dawning. "Identification. Fake alien registration cards, things like that."

"Maybe." He looked at her closely. "Hard to say. But if your friend Jill was onto something about these people — she was in the right place at the right time. And if she had information about what was happening about these refugees, then maybe she was right to feel hunted."

"By whom, though?"

Manny shrugged and wiped his mouth with a napkin. "Our guys, their guys — doesn't really matter anymore. This country's been getting tighter and tighter on restricting political asylum. A kinder, gentler nation — what a load of shit."

"And getting sent back to El Salvador is the same thing as walking down the hall to the gas chamber." Helen tasted her cold coffee, made a face. "I don't know. It makes a certain kind of sense, but it's pretty far-fetched."

"Helen." Manny pushed his plate aside and leaned forward, speaking softly. "Has it crossed your mind that . . . well, that the phone message you describe sounds a little bit like the kind of things she was saying when they picked her up in Calexico? The stuff about CIA and FBI agents after her?"

"You mean you think she was crazy."

"I don't know if I mean that. Hell, I'm crazier than most people we know. And we won't even start on you."

"I know how it sounds, Manny. Believe me, Frieda and I have been going around and around with this since Sunday morning, when we first saw the newspaper story." Helen set the mug to one side and waved the waitress away. "But I have to make sure. I owe it to her."

He nodded. "You owe it to her. But why? Can you tell me that?"

Helen thought of the late night calls, the demands for money, food, a shoulder to cry on. "I can't explain. I just have to be sure."

"Suit yourself, Watson." Helen watched him dig in his billfold for a few bills. He reared back in the booth in mock surprise. "What? You're not going to fight me for the bill, like any red-blooded Berkeley feminist?"

"Not today," she answered, sliding out from the booth. "You owe me for about a thousand meals. Besides, you forgot — I'm paying for a stay at this marvelous resort hotel in the beautiful hills of the East Bay."

"Nothing but the best, eh?"

Helen rolled her eyes. "Well, if the best is a sort of Holiday Inn meets the Sex Pistols."

"You're dating yourself, Watson. They went out of fashion about fifteen years ago. Where you headed now?"

"Oh, places."

"Getting into more trouble?"

124

"I hope not. No, it's more like — like last rites for a friend."

She left him waving at her, then turned around and headed west to San Pablo Dam Road. St. Bonaventure's was only minutes away.

Chapter Sixteen

Helen, having been raised as an anti-papist in the deep south, had no idea what was going on in St. Bonaventure's when she crept into one of the back pews. A few other stragglers hung about the back of the church, sidling sheepishly along the shadowy rows near the door. A white-robed priest knelt before the altar, head bowed. When he rose and turned to address the people gathered, he spoke in Spanish. Helen kneeled forward and saw that most of the small group crowded into the front were Hispanic. When the priest lifted his hands over the bowed congregation in a final solemn blessing, his long ponytail, oddly out of place with the vestments, slipped out from beneath the green ribbon-like garment he wore across his shoulders to swing down across his chest. Helen could not be certain, but his build and height certainly matched that of the man she'd seen in the woods the night before.

When he had finished his prayer and the people had crossed themselves, Helen edged her way along the side of the church, staying close to the wall. She scanned the fifteen or so people gathered around the priest and was soon rewarded with the sight of Marta's thin anxious features looking up at his averted face. Marta and the priest were talking in low tense whispers. As Marta shook her head vehemently at him, she caught a glimpse of Helen standing beneath a statue of the Virgin. The girl's eyes widened in fear and, with a sharp pull at the priest's sleeve, she stood staring at Helen. The priest turned. Helen immediately felt the power of his gaze. The small black eyes held little of what Helen would have called Christian charity, but she was sure that righteous zeal was one of his traits.

There was nothing else to be done now. Helen put on what she hoped was a broad smile and walked forward to meet them. Marta managed to hide her feelings enough to nod a greeting. The priest's smile and extended hand did nothing to alter his hard eyes.

Introductions were stiff. "Marta says you're staying at Still Waters Lodge. How awful for you, to have such a thing happen," Father John Hitchcock said in a voice that was a little too casual, all the while boring into her with those black eyes.

"Yes, it was terrible, Father," Helen answered. "Especially since I knew Jill Gallagher."

"Oh?" He took a step closer. The red light shimmering behind the altar was blocked out by his height. "I'm so sorry about her. You must be very sad."

"Yes, especially since she won't get to finish her story now." Both Father John and Marta grew very still at her words. It had been a long shot, connecting Jill and Marta, but their reaction told Helen that she had hit dead center. They glanced at each other, and Helen heard Marta's sharp intake of breath.

"Then she was involved in writing another article when she died?" He smiled and shook his head gently. "I'm afraid I know very little about her work," he said.

Like hell you don't, Helen thought. She went on, "Yes, she had just returned from Central America, I believe."

Marta, who had stayed quiet throughout this interchange, heaved a huge sigh. Helen thought she heard her mutter *"Madre de Dios"* but she might have imagined it. Father John ignored her and made a motion with one arm as if he were trying to usher Helen away. He himself began to edge down the aisle. "How interesting. Yes, it's a pity."

"By the way, Father," Helen said, following him, "I get this feeling I've seen you somewhere before. Maybe you've come by the hotel, to visit Marta?"

He halted only for a moment in his progress through the central aisle of the church. "Yes," he answered, speaking slowly, "I try to keep on very friendly terms with all my parishioners. I often visit them where they work as well as where they live."

"That must have been it, then. I could have sworn I'd seen you somewhere before. I think it might have even been last night, but it was pretty dark out in the woods. I can't be too sure."

The priest's expression became blank.

Helen turned around to get a glimpse of how the girl was taking all this and immediately regretted it. At once she felt ashamed of her obsessive need to search out the truth. Marta stood alone, next to the altar, visibly shaking. One hand clutched the other as she strained to understand what Helen and Father John were saying, but she was too afraid to approach them.

Helen turned to the doors ahead of her, eager to get away from the church, to get away from the disgust that suddenly overwhelmed her. Father John stood still and silent, waiting for her next verbal volley. Embarrassed by her own behavior, Helen started for the door.

"Nice to meet you, Father. See you later, Marta." She was nearly at the last pew. If she hadn't been focusing on Marta and the priest, Helen would have noticed the half-open door to the confessional gradually opening wider as she passed by.

Everything happened very quickly — the lunging figure emerging from the dark confessional, the gleaming flash of the knife in a hand that held it high, the piercing scream that seemed to swell endlessly from Marta. For some reason that afterward Helen never could understand or explain, the carved image of Jesus bending beneath the cross, his face bruised and bloodied, held her eye as she felt the cold sting of sharp metal on her throat. She heard Father John's heavy step once, then twice, as he stopped a few feet behind her assailant. "No, Jose. No," he was saying in a fierce whisper.

A strange voice vibrated with anger. "I'll kill the bitch!" it quavered as two steely arms pressed her close. "No one can make me go back. No one!"

Helen pretended to relax in the arms of her assailant. As she sensed him easing up on the pressure, she shoved her right elbow back as hard as she could. She got him in the belly, and he doubled over in surprise and pain. She turned and elbowed him again, this time in the lower back. He howled out in pain at the blow to his kidneys. Helen knelt on his back and wrenched the knife from his outstretched palm.

He put up no more resistance, and now that she got a good look at him, his frailty was clear. Quickly she got up and grabbed him under the arms. With Father John's help she managed to heave him into the nearest pew. All the while Marta was huddled near a statue of the Virgin, her hands clutched to her mouth.

Helen flopped down on the pew next to the priest. "You want to tell me what the hell is going on here, Father?"

At first he ignored her. "Don't worry, Marta. He'll be fine." This was followed by a few phrases in Spanish that seemed to comfort her. He stood up, supporting the man in his arms. "You want to give me a hand?" he asked Helen.

Helen felt too tired to be surprised at the way

this day was turning out. Without a word she offered her shoulder.

The trio followed Marta down a narrow corridor that led from the back of the church to a small office. As soon as they'd deposited their burden in a chair, Marta flew off down the hall. The priest stripped off his vestments to reveal a plain button-down shirt and black slacks. Helen found a chair in front of the desk that filled most of the room. Father John sat down at the desk. They remained silent until Marta returned, carrying a sponge and a small basin.

"This is Jose, Marta's husband." He broke the silence so suddenly that Helen jumped. "I'm sure you've figured out where he's from."

Helen felt a twinge of pain in her neck every time she turned her head to see the dark young man who sat to her left. He kept tipping his straight-backed chair against the wall, making the books stacked loosely on the metal utility shelves shift and nudge each other. Marta never took her eyes off him. She stood with her back to the door of the stuffy little room, her hands knotted behind her as she watched everyone and everything with quiet intensity.

Father John was the only one who looked relaxed. He leaned back in his ancient swivel chair and tapped his fingertips on the desk. "Maybe if you'd been chased and beaten and tortured by a gang of thugs, you wouldn't react too well at being followed yet again."

"I'm not out to do anything to Jose or to Marta," Helen protested in irritation. "A friend of mine just got killed, and all I'm trying to do is find out what happened to her."

"A friend of yours got killed. Just like these two have seen hundreds — no, thousands, killed for speaking out and trying to change things in their country." The priest got up suddenly and paced back and forth in the narrow strip between his desk and the wall, jamming his fists in his pockets. His face looked old and tired in the odd shadows cast by the light on the desk. "There's no reason to involve them in the investigation. I can tell you they had nothing to do with it, nothing! They were just in the wrong place at the wrong time."

He walked around the desk, and leaned uncomfortably close to Helen, looming over her like a predatory bird. "Do you know what will happen to Jose if the police find him and start questioning him? Until I can get him out of the state, to someplace safe, his life is in danger. He'll be shipped right back to El Salvador by the paranoid schizophrenics we have running this country. Right back to a firing squad. Now, do you want to be responsible for that?"

"Look, if I was so interested in getting Jose in trouble, do you think I would have come here all alone? I know you must be smarter than that, Father." Helen let that sink in for a moment, then went on more quietly. "I just want to find out what happened the night Jill died. I know she had found your shack —"

"Damn!" He got up from the desk and began prowling around the room. "And how did you find out?"

"Let's just say I followed some clues she left

132

behind. If I could find it, then it won't be too hard for the police, or the immigration people, or whoever it is you're hiding from, would it?" Helen looked from one to the other, waiting for a response.

"It's okay," Marta said, reaching up to stop Father John. She turned to Helen, defeat sinking into her face. "That's why we were moving the stuff out last night when you saw us."

"What stuff?"

"For identification. Alien registration cards, work permits, drivers' licenses," Father John burst out. He slumped down into his chair. "That's the place they were using."

Marta said to Helen, "But Father John had nothing to do with it. He only knew that Jose was here. It was . . . other people. People who try to help us."

"And somehow Jill found out about all this." Helen sat silent, thinking it through. Somehow, in her trip to El Salvador, Jill must have caught on to the work these people were doing. "That's why she was staying at the hotel."

"I don't know how she found out about all this," Marta said, shaking her head. "She started to ask me a lot of questions, and I got scared. So I call Father to please help us." She turned aside to say something to her husband, who hadn't stopped glaring at Helen since they'd entered the room. "It was time to move, anyway. We — my friends and me — we don't like to stay too long with all that equipment in one place."

"Don't worry, Marta. I don't want to know who your friends are. Like I said, I just want to know what happened to Jill."

"Why don't you take Jose up to the guest room, Marta? I think he's had enough for one night."

Father John helped her out the door. Jose threw one final glare at Helen before leaving, then Helen was alone with the priest. She was silent, waiting for him to talk.

"So, now what?" he finally said. "Are you going to get in touch with the authorities?"

Helen shook her head. "I don't see any reason why I should, right now. At least I know for sure what it was Jill was after. Whether that has any bearing on her death — who knows? It gives me something to work with. At last." She got up to leave, but the priest was still blocking the door. Helen saw again how tall, how strong he was.

"How commendable. I suppose if it served your purposes, you'd turn them in without a second thought? As long as you got your precious information."

"If I thought they had any responsibility for Jill's death — yes. Murder is murder, no matter who does it."

"Even if it meant the lives of thousands of people?" He towered over her, and Helen felt her body tensing for another attack. "Do you have any idea what her story would have done to these people? Their lives depend on secrecy. That woman was about to blow the whole thing — signing their death warrants for the sake of good publicity."

"I thought Marta said you weren't involved."

He backed away to the desk. "I care. These people matter to God, and to me. I'm not going to stand by and watch them be destroyed by thoughtless, self-seeking idiots who don't care about anything but money."

Helen leaned against the door, drained of all energy. When she spoke her voice was distant, tired. "I happen to believe Jill Gallagher mattered to your God just as much as Marta and Jose do. And I'm going to do everything I can to find out who killed her. Whether you like it or not."

She was out of the room before he could say another word.

Chapter Seventeen

Helen shielded her eyes from the sun that streamed a final few rays over the hills and onto the lake. The wind and rain that had blanketed the area had been swept away in a brief, brilliant burst of light and warmth that foretold the beginning of summer.

As soon as Helen had returned from St. Bonaventure's, Frieda had suggested a walk along the shore of Still Waters Lake, complaining that unless she got some fresh air and got away from all those people, she'd go nuts. Now they were walking along the white sand, maintaining a respectable distance between their bodies, although Helen couldn't help noticing the way the afternoon sun brought out the reddish tints of Frieda's hair.

"You've done a lot today," she said to Frieda with a smile. "A lot more than anything I achieved." Frieda bowed in mock solemnity while Helen perused the notes. "Your idea was right."

"Like I said — doing sketches of people is a good way to get them to talk about themselves. They're so excited to see how lovely they are, how interested I am in their unusual features, that they can't resist me."

"Well, I sure can't resist you. I find you overwhelming."

"Good." Frieda started to say something else, then tensed when she saw that they were nearly at the group of rocks where Jill had met her death. She shivered and pulled Helen's jacket around her more closely.

"Too cold? Want to go back?"

"No, I'm fine," she said, resolute. "This jacket is great — I can't think why I never borrowed it from you before."

"Let's sit down and take a look at this." Helen chose a broad flat surface that seemed clear from any protruding bumps or edges, and sat facing the lake, her back to the wall that reached up to the highway. Far above they could hear cars and trucks groaning up the incline, the noise muted by the wind and the gentle murmur of water moving across sand.

As if reading her thoughts, Frieda said, "It's so hard to imagine what happened here a few nights

137

ago. It seems so peaceful — as if there were no one else around. Just you and me."

Helen touched her hand briefly, then studied her notes again. Frieda's writing, so much neater than her own, outlined information in neat rows across the pale gray sheet torn from her sketch pad:

Chester and Louise Palmer: tucked away in
    bed on the night in question
Alex and Amy O'Neill: same as the Palmers
The McKendricks: husband off in D.C., Mom
    and kids at the movies, then to bed
Mr. Benson: covering the desk until after
    midnight while Miranda away
Miranda Benson: staying with her sister out
    of town

"We can add Marta's name to the list." Helen scrawled a few words below Frieda's notes. "Says she was in Berkeley, with the priest that night. So they can back each other up."

"You mean you don't believe her?"

"It's him, more than her. The man is a fanatic, I don't care what kind of vows he's taken. Jill had somehow gotten hold of their network — the way they got refugees up to the States, into safety. I'm sure that was the big story she was working on."

"But surely she would have kept everyone anonymous, not given out details in what she wrote. I mean, journalists are supposed to protect their sources, right?"

"Sure, in the best of all possible worlds. But how could Father John, or Marta, really know for sure? Jill had traced them to the spot where they made

138

false documents. She was that close to knowing the whole thing." Helen shrugged and squinted out across the lake, mesmerized by the play of light on the water. Soon it would be dark. "They would have seen it as protecting hundreds of people from death if they got rid of her."

"It's just difficult to believe a Catholic priest could do such a thing."

Helen laughed. "If you'd run into as many fanatics as I have, you'd know they're capable of just about anything. Of course, they didn't have too many Catholics where I come from — mostly fundamentalists. Even a few that handled snakes in their worship."

Frieda grimaced in distaste. "Remind me not to go to church with you if we ever visit the folks in Mississippi."

"I doubt they'd let us past the front door. You don't have anything to worry about —" Helen broke off as Frieda's face darkened. "What is it?"

Frieda was holding a tattered slip of paper in her hand, poring over it with intensity. "This was in your jacket. In the pocket," she said in strange dull tones.

"Well, what is it? Let me see." She took it from Frieda, who offered it without resistance. Puzzled, Helen made out the words: "Come see me at eight o'clock tonight. My place. Be sure to leave Mama at home — I'll make it worth your while. J."

Helen's brow cleared after a few moments of consternation. "My God, I'd forgotten all about this. Jill gave me this note last October, six months ago." She sighed and shook her head, still holding the note loosely in her hand. "Begging for money again, as usual. It was always so pathetic, the way she — Frieda, what's wrong with you?"

Frieda's voice had grown as cold as the wind that followed the sinking sun. "Why didn't you ever tell me that you were seeing her?"

"Seeing her? Frieda, I wasn't *seeing* her. I mean, when I did talk to her she just wanted money, or favors. Jill was practically out on the street a few times during the last couple of years. All I ever did was help her out. You can't really imagine anything else was going on!"

"It would explain a lot. Why you feel so compelled to chase imaginary murderers in Contra Costa County. Why you're so torn up about her death that you can't even talk to me about it." The face that Frieda turned to meet Helen's gaze was as white as the sand that encircled the rocks.

"You really think I was sleeping with Jill? Risking our relationship for a quick fuck with someone I felt sorry for? Come on, Frieda." The events of the day — the fight with Jose, the confrontation with Amy, visiting Jill's apartment — all these had drained Helen, leaving her no energy to fight down the anger in her voice. "That's utterly ridiculous."

"Is it? How do I know? I do my best to respect your privacy. I keep a safe distance so you won't get spooked. But I can't stand the way you put me in a hermetically sealed compartment, Helen. Jesus, I'm your lover! We've been together for eight years, we live together, and I still don't know you." She clambered down the rocks and stood below Helen, surrounded by shadow. "I just wish you had told me."

140

"Frieda, there was nothing to tell. What are we fighting about?"

"We're not fighting about anything, because I'm going back." She turned on her heel, kicking up a shallow spray of sand behind her, and trudged back to the path that led to the hotel.

Helen watched her go, nearly calling her back. Instead she scrambled down off of the rocks to follow her.

They walked along in silence, Helen staying a few paces in back of Frieda, whose face cooled from anger into a distant thoughtfulness. It was Frieda who spoke first. "Why did you want me to come along with you to the hotel, Helen?"

"Well, I wanted you with me. I always want you with me," Helen said lamely.

Frieda smiled sadly and shook her head. "If I remember correctly, I pretty much invited myself along, didn't I? Tagging along like the annoying kid sister who's always in the way. You should have refused."

"Hey, now." Helen caught up with her in two steps. The breeze had blown the hair across Frieda's face, and Helen brushed away the loose strands with her fingers, the touch turning into a brief caress. "I would never do that. I love you, Frieda. You're part of my life."

"Am I?" Frieda stood still, looking out over the water. "I wonder sometimes."

"How could you possibly wonder that?"

"I wonder every time I find out little secrets about you. Little pieces of information you thought I shouldn't know about. Like the way you wouldn't tell me you've been seeing Jill. How long was that going

141

on? Months? Years?" Frieda's voice stayed calm, but her eyes were full of pain and loneliness.

"Frieda, believe me, there was nothing going on. Jill was usually too far gone with alcohol whenever I saw her to make an affair possible! You know how she was —"

"No. I don't know how she was. You never saw fit to tell me." By now they had reached the path. On either side the trees loomed up, blocking out the last rays of the sun. The trail looked ominous in the sudden gloom. Frieda turned away from Helen, seemingly preoccupied with kicking at a few loose pebbles at her feet. Finally she said, "How many other things do you keep hidden from me?"

Helen sighed as she leaned against a thick trunk that jabbed up waist high at the edge of the sand. She shuddered with the cold, wishing she could somehow persuade Frieda to continue this in the warmth of the hotel. "There was no need for you to know about it. You're making a mountain out of the proverbial molehill about the whole thing. And how you can think I don't love you, especially after last night —"

"This has nothing to do with sex, and you know it, Helen." Frieda's fragile temper snapped. Her voice remained quiet, but her eyes flashed with anger. "Yeah, I'm good for a quick fuck anytime you feel like it, but as far as telling me anything, I'm just not worth it. Isn't that it?"

"What is it — do you want to know every little detail of my life, for Christ's sake? Do I have to check in with you whenever I take a dump, for example? My God, Frieda, we're not prisoners."

"So that's how I make you feel."

"Whenever you pressure me about my private life, yes."

"Your private life. I see. Your life apart from me."

Helen stood up, feeling the strange sense of rightness that signalled an acknowledgement of truth, no matter how unwelcome. "I guess that's true. I do feel I have a part of my life that has nothing to do with you. It's not bigger or more important than the part I share with you, but it does exist."

Frieda nodded. The shadows were by now so deep that Helen couldn't make out the expression on Frieda's face — it was just a dark oval. "Maybe that's why I insisted on coming with you here," Frieda said in a tired, flat voice. "I wanted to prove to myself that it wasn't true."

"That what wasn't true?"

"What I've suspected ever since you started the agency — the fact that I'm just not important enough to you to make a difference in your life."

In the cover of darkness Helen felt safe enough to reach out and try to take her lover in her arms. "You are important, Frieda. What we have is enough for me. Does it have to be any more?"

Frieda was stiff and unyielding in her embrace. Helen finally gave up, releasing her. They stood at arms' length, watching each other for what seemed like hours. "Maybe it's not enough for me, Helen. I don't know yet."

Helen was hardly aware of how they got up the path back to the hotel after that, but she was aware of light diffusing through the thinning trees, her feet on the stones, the lessening of the cold wind blowing off the lake. Neither she nor Frieda said another word. The only sound was the bending and twisting of branches, the grinding of pebbles in the path.

Then, as they emerged on the other side, Helen heard another noise. She knew, before she could actually see the source, what it was. The scratchy monotone, the numbers rattled out dispassionately, the buzz of static. She stopped, and Frieda stopped with her.

Helen turned to her in surprise. "The police are here."

Chapter Eighteen

The two women walked into a scene that might have been taken directly from a situation comedy. The patrol car, emblazoned with the garish emblem of Contra Costa County Sheriff's Department, blocked the way for other vehicles to pass across the wide pavement at the entrance to the lobby. Just in front of it was another car.

"That's not the van that belongs to the priest, is it?" Frieda asked Helen.

Helen squeezed by the sheriff's car and peered

down at the van's license plate. "The very same. This is getting interesting."

Frieda leaned against the van. Her face was pale and drawn.

Helen said, "Care to call a truce long enough to find out what's going on?"

"You never give up, do you?" Frieda broke into a shaky laugh. "Why not?"

"Come on." They entered the lobby and were met by a cacophony of voices. Louise and Chester Palmer were holding court, wearing their standard matching sweatsuits, this time in hot pink. Even their mall-walkers were studded with patches of pink fabric. The color did nothing for either, especially since Louise's face was a bright fire-engine red. Chester stood stoically by while Louise screeched in a blaring voice meant for everyone's ears.

"I'm not going to shut up until we get to the bottom of this!" she bleated. "It happens every time we have to be in the same place with a spic —"

Benson shook his head vehemently as she leaned over the counter, his hands flat on the surface as if it was the only thing holding him up. Helen was shocked at his appearance. In the few hours since she'd first seen him he had visibly weakened. She wondered if he'd had any sleep for the past few days. "Mrs. Palmer, there's no call for that kind of talk. I'll have to ask you to —"

She cut him off, jabbing a finger at him, nearly poking him in his flabby chest. "Don't you interrupt me! I still got plenty to say. And Chester will back me up on this, won't you, Chester?"

Chester stood up straighter, harumphed, and tried to give an impression of a resolute, sturdy

146

member of the male species, but his jaw was clearly trembling.

In the center of the room, Officer Bowles presided. Legs apart, he planted his size tens firmly onto the thick pile carpet as if he expected to be rooted there for the night. His back was turned to Helen and Frieda as they entered the room. "Now, just what exactly is the problem, ma'am?" he intoned in a carefully studied drawl.

The finger moved away from Benson, who dodged it in passing, and pointed to the far side of the lobby. "That spic over there stole my wallet!"

Marta was sitting on a low chair in front of the fireplace, her small body huddled in misery. Standing behind her was Father John Hitchcock, his hands protectively placed on the back of the chair. He watched Helen and Frieda as they entered the room but gave no sign of recognition beyond a faint flicker in his eyes. Marta was too absorbed in her dilemma to notice anyone but her accuser.

Benson said soothingly, "Mrs. Palmer, I simply can't believe this. There must be some sort of mistake, some misunderstanding. Marta just isn't the type of person —"

"Oh, I know how it is with you people," Louise hissed. "You just hire these illegals so they'll work cheap. You don't know a doggone thing about them — where they come from, if they're liars, cheaters, whores, whatever."

Father John stirred from his position, anger in every movement. "Marta, you don't have to stay here and listen to any of this," he said. "This is outrageous. Officer, surely you can see that this woman is hysterical?"

147

"Hysterical? Hysterical? I'll show you hysterical, mister, unless I get my wallet back!"

At that moment a thin shaft of light beamed across the counter as Miranda Benson looked out from the office behind the registration area.

"It's okay, honey," Benson murmured to her. He glanced at the Palmers nervously and made a stab at his usual hearty chuckle. "Just a little misunderstanding, that's all."

"Misunderstanding!" Louise huffed, her mouth dropping open in round astonishment.

"But what is it, Dad? Sounds like World War Three." Miranda stood halfway out of the room, one arm holding the door open. The light shone through her hair, and Helen felt a tug of recognition. She searched her pockets for the photograph she'd picked up in Jill's apartment. Marta said something in Spanish, just a soft murmur. When Miranda responded in the same language, Helen knew for certain.

"What did she say?" Louise started across the room and Miranda stepped out of the office and darted out from behind the counter. "What are you two talking about?"

"She's frightened, Mrs. Palmer," Miranda said, obviously reining in her temper. "She says she had nothing to do with it. Whatever 'it' is." She looked back at her father, waiting for some kind of explanation. "I don't think she understands what's going on."

"Don't let that innocent look fool you. They always understand more than they let on."

"Mrs. Palmer has mislaid her wallet —"

"Had it stolen you mean!"

148

Benson tried again. "Her wallet is missing. Apparently she feels that Marta had something to do with it, but I've been trying to tell Jim here that it's all a mistake."

"That's impossible. Marta would never do such a thing." Miranda went to the accused girl and put an arm around her shoulder, speaking softly to her in Spanish.

Louise said loudly to Officer Bowles, "She's the only person, besides my husband and myself, who's had access to that room, so I don't see why we're waiting around anymore. Arrest that whore!"

"Now, ma'am, unless you can prove something, I'm not sure there's anything I can do."

"This is outrageous! I'm an American citizen! I have rights!" Louise plunked down into the nearest chair, which shuddered under her.

Officer Bowles sighed deeply. "Well, I guess I have to write out a report, Benson," he said, taking his clipboard over to the registration counter. Unhappily Benson made room for him, sliding a stack of receipts and the telephone out of his way.

Helen watched Father John pacing the room, muttering, "I can't believe the ignorance — just crazy." Suddenly he broke from his walk and joined Bowles at the counter, saying to Benson, "May I use your phone, sir?" He punched at the numbers rapidly. "Bob? It's John Hitchcock. Listen, I've got a little problem here. We have a young lady who's going to need some help. Can you spare — Well, I'm not sure."

The conversation went on in muted tones while Bowles took down information from the Palmers. Father John hung up just as the deputy was turning

149

to Marta. "She doesn't have to say anything to you, Officer. Marta, we're getting a lawyer from the free legal aid office to meet us tonight —"

"Listen, Rev, all I want is to get name, address, that kind of thing. Just keep your collar on." Bowles looked down at Marta and Helen saw the odd smile that stole over his face without reaching his steely eyes. "I'm sure the lady would like to cooperate. Wouldn't she?"

Helen wondered if anyone besides herself saw the way Marta slumped in the chair in an eloquent sign of defeat. Bowles kept staring at her, and the grin got bigger. The young woman's face became smooth and blank. "Of course I will help."

"Let's see your alien registration card."

Marta shook her head at the priest's protests and listlessly rummaged around in her shoulder bag, which she'd slung over the back of her chair. As she stood up to give him the square of plastic, a black leather clutch wallet fell out of the bag onto the floor.

Louise shrieked in triumph. "What did I tell you? She took it, just like I said! See?" She was across the room in a moment, crouching on the floor, her shaking hands flipping through the piles of credit cards, counting the bills. "I guess she didn't take anything," Louise muttered, disappointed. "But that's only because she didn't have time to."

"I'm afraid there's more to it than that," Bowles said. He tapped a finger on the card Marta had given him, no longer trying to hide the grin. "I have to say, this card looks pretty fake to me, ma'am." He scribbled a few more notes on the sheet of paper, dotted a couple of i's with vigor. "Looks like you're living here illegally, Miss. I'll have to ask you to come down to the station with me."

The next few moments were a confusion of various sounds — Father John angrily shouting as he gestured at the deputy, Miranda joining her father back at the counter and imploring him to do something, Louise crowing with delight at her victory, as if in one fell swoop she'd saved the American way of life.

But it was Marta who Helen watched as she stood up, showing no more fear, only a quiet acceptance. "It's okay, it's okay," she kept repeating to the priest. "It will be all right."

Father John was back on the telephone, while Miranda and her father tried to talk to Bowles. He paid no attention to them, but calmly put his pen back in his pocket, stuck the clipboard under his arm and turned back to Marta. With a courtly deference just short of mockery he gestured politely for her to precede him. After one long look into his eyes she did so. Father John slammed the phone down for the second time as they walked out the door. "Damn!" he whispered, then tried another number.

Outside, Bowles laughed. "You're dumber than I thought, Marta, for taking that wallet."

"I did not take it," she sighed, leaning against the door of the patrol car. "You know that."

"How the hell would I know? Maybe you figured on stealing that broad's money to get you and that beaner husband of yours lit out for the territories.

151

Maybe," he breathed, moving up close against her, "maybe you was trying to get away from me, too. That wouldn't have gone through that pretty little head of yours, would it?" He began to gyrate his hips slowly against hers. With one hand he reached for the handle of the door. "I think we should have a little talk about this."

"Where are you taking me?"

"Don't you worry about that, young lady." He put one hand on top of her head and shoved her unceremoniously into the car. "We got our own private little third degree to get through. Just you and me, honey, in our secret sugar shack." He whistled as he rounded the car to the driver's seat. Marta stole a look at the van as they pulled away, then ducked her eyes down again quickly.

For just one brief moment, she imagined she had seen movement in the back window of the van — a flash of white shirt, a glint of dark eyes, from the place where she knew her husband had been hiding.

As soon as the driveway was silent, the back door of the van creaked open. Jose dropped nimbly to the ground and crept up to the front of the vehicle. He made very little noise as he climbed into the driver's seat. It didn't take him long to hotwire the van and get it out to the main highway. Bowles had disappeared, but Jose was pretty sure where the cop had taken his wife.

Chapter Nineteen

The patrol car bumped and jerked its way along the unpaved trail that led off the main road. Officer Bowles had driven this way often before over the course of the last few months, so he knew each twist of the steering wheel, each pothole that required deceleration. Marta tossed in the back seat, quiet and dull, paying little attention to the details of scenery. He eased the car to a stop no more than ten yards away from the tool shed that Helen had found the previous night. As before, it was deserted, as still and isolated as if it had never been used.

Switching off the ignition, Bowles grunted in surprise. "They musta towed the bitch's car away." He waited a moment, tapping his palms on the wheel in time to his own private melody. The car's absence unsettled him, but it took him only a few moments to make up his mind. "Come on, Marta. Let's you and me take a look around."

When she sat still in the car, ignoring his order, he wrenched open the back door and yanked her out. She flinched at the pain, which only made him laugh. "Whatsa matter, too dark? Can't start screaming or crying now, can you?"

"What are you going to do? Why are we here?" she whispered, although there was no one else present to hear her words. Bowles gripped her arm tight, stumbling her along after him. He bent over to duck his head as they entered the shed, shoving her in front of him, and switching on the lights. Marta couldn't prevent a small cry of pain when her knee crashed into the sharp edge of a metal table. He stood over her and looked around the room with a proprietary air.

"Where'd all your stuff go, Marta? Pawnshop? Did you give it away? Or did you pull up operations, think you could just skedaddle without saying boo to anyone? Huh?" His foot prodded her, still gentle, still teasing; he was not yet worked up to the point of kicking her. She made not a sound, not a move, knowing too well that it would only provoke him to further demonstrations of his power over her.

He crouched down next to her, so close that she could smell the sweat that had soaked and then dried on his uniform all day. "Have you forgotten something, sweetheart? All you shitkickers think you can get away with something without me knowing it. Well, don't you forget one thing, baby. I can hurt you good." He grabbed her by the shoulders and pulled her up off the floor. "I can ship you right back to El Salvador anytime I fucking well like it. Got it?"

Their eyes were inches apart, and somehow he was able to read the hatred in her gaze. It infuriated him. He slapped her. "Better yet," he said, "I can tell your husband what we've been doing, night after night. Just you and me, fucking like a pair of rabbits. How do you think that man of yours would feel about that, huh? He's likely to kill you for it."

At the mention of her husband, Marta's fear changed to rage. With one violent jerk of her head she spat in his face. Bowles gasped, shocked and utterly unprepared. His retaliation was swift and complete. Two blows to her jaw and she was down, nearly unconscious, but still trying to crawl away from him. He grabbed her leg and pulled her back as he wiped her spittle from his cheek. "Just what the fuck do you think I am? Jesus H. Christ, you'll pay for that one, cunt."

Once again she was flat on her back while he stood over her, one foot on either side of her body. Head cocked to one side, he looked down, regarding her as if she were a curiosity in a zoo. "I kinda like it when you fight back, you know? Makes it more fun." He pulled a pack of cigarettes out of his shirt pocket. " 'Sides, I haven't beat anyone up for a while. Things were getting kind of dull."

The plastic wrapping on the packet made a noise as loud as drums in Marta's ears. She opened her eyes to watch the flame from the match travel in midair to the end of his cigarette, then saw the tiny red embers glowing. For just a moment she thought she saw something else — a face in the window, a blank circle just staring — then she decided she must be hallucinating. It had happened to her before, more than once, when she'd been stuck in the hell of a prison outside San Salvador. The vision disappeared almost as quickly as it had come, and she regretted its passing. It meant that she was indeed conscious and aware, and in for a terrible time, the outcome of which she could only guess.

The tiny dot of light that marked Bowles' cigarette moved up and down, up and down, and the scent of smoke filled the room. The next sound Marta heard was an odd, metallic rip. It took a moment for her to identify it as a zipper. Something about its prosaic quality startled her into hysterical giggling.

"Think it's funny, do you?" Bowles carefully set his gun and holster down on the floor. He was breathing heavily. "It's like I always said — bitches love it when you treat 'em rough, no matter what they say." His hands pushed her legs apart and then her clothes were being ripped. Too sore, too exhausted to be afraid any longer, Marta willed herself to become a blank, far away from the present moment.

In fact, at first when the door burst open, she believed she was in some kind of trance state, lost in a dream of wishful thinking. It wasn't until her body registered the removal of Bowles' weight from her that she realized something was happening. Cold air from the outside world rushed in and blew all the smoke out of the shed. Its chill roused her and she leaned up on one elbow, trying to understand what was happening.

"Jose?" she whispered tremulously. "Jose?"

Her husband stood just inside the door, panting for air. He was black against the silvery stretch of forest framed by the doorway, while the moon streamed in behind him. Marta could see that his hands hung empty by his sides. Fear took her over again — fear not for herself, but for him.

She spoke to him in Spanish. "Jose, he'll kill you. Please, please don't do this."

He cut her off. "Get back to the church. Find Father John. I will meet you there soon."

"But, Jose —"

"Do it!"

All the while this brief interchange was going on, Bowles glared from one to the other of them. He was by no means fluent in Spanish, but he had no trouble interpreting what was going on. He was surprised, but still in control. "This must be the lucky man, huh, Marta?"

He laughed and reached for his holster, only to have his hand scratch and claw at the splintery wood of the floor. Marta had slid out of his way just in time, managing to toss the holster into the farthest corner of the room.

"You little cunt — bitch —" He spewed out curses as he went for her, but the moment was all Marta needed. Somehow her legs found strength, and she scrambled to the door next to Jose before Bowles could get his pants back up over his knees.

He lunged at Jose. "You motherfucking bastard — you'll get it now. I got plans for you." Bowles

157

barreled over a broken chair and the metal table in his way. Jose sidestepped him and then watched him trip over his own feet. As Bowles regained his footing, grabbing at the walls for balance, Jose turned to find Marta poised near the door, ready for flight.

"Go, now!"

"Please, you have to come with me, Jose," Marta pleaded. She reached out a shaking hand to touch him. He stood, frozen with hate, unable to feel her touch. "This will only end in something awful, I know it. We must get out of here."

Instead of trying to answer her, Jose blindly pushed her away.

Bowles, on his feet, was snorting like a bull, huffing in huge gulps of air, so overcome by amazement that he sputtered when he tried to talk. "God, I am going to enjoy ripping you apart, you goddam greaser! Come on in here and get it, boy!"

Marta put her hands to her head, as if to squeeze out all thought, all vision of what was happening. Jose heard her scream. He shouted, "Get out! Do it! Find Father John!" Then he turned back to face Bowles.

The deputy had managed to find his gun, but after weighing it in his hand for a moment he turned it over as if not certain what to do with it. Looking down intently at it, he sneered, "I can't quite figure out whether to kill you like a dog or give you the beating you got coming to you." He looked at Marta. "You watching this, baby?"

Jose said, "I'll make it easy for you." He moved while Bowles stared at Marta. A blow came ringing down on the police officer's head and he dropped his gun as red, black and green lights flashed and faded before his dazzled eyes. When the spots cleared, Bowles saw the two-by-four in Jose's hand. Jose held it high over his head, preparing to strike him again. Bowles was retching from the pain, but he managed to avoid the makeshift weapon by rolling under the metal table. The board hit the thin surface with a clang that rang painfully in his already ringing ears. He crawled out from under the table and groped for the gun on the floor.

Jose pushed into the shed, tossing the few remaining stools, chairs, and table out of his way. He'd almost expended the temporary strength given him by a rush of adrenalin. Physical weakness brought on by months of maltreatment in El Salvadoran prisons revealed itself in an uncontrollable shaking of his limbs. He swung out again at Bowles with the two-by-four, but missed in a huge sweeping arc. The board smashed through the filthy glass of the window beside the deputy's head.

"Missed me, beaner," Bowles chuckled, getting to his feet. He was calm now, although one eye was swollen shut. "Now I got me some target practice." Jose saw the dull gleam of the gun as Bowles gestured with it. "Up against the wall, shithead. Go on, move." As Jose passed by him, he got in a swift kick, toppling the smaller man over beneath the broken window. "Whoops! You got to be more careful how you get around. You might hurt yourself sometime." Other than Jose's ragged breathing, the only sound was the soft snick of the safety on

159

Bowles' gun. "Take a good look," he breathed, leaning in close. "This is the last thing you'll ever see."

Bowles felt himself filling with cold pleasure as he lowered the gun towards Jose's face. Suddenly the shadowy figure below him moved. Then there was a steadily increasing pain in his gut. Puzzled, he put a hand to his belly and felt warm moisture, which spread over his fingers with amazing rapidity. He took his hand away from his body and held it up to his eyes. A few drops of blood fell to the floor.

"What the —" Bowles looked down and finally saw the long shard of broken glass from the window that Jose had plunged into his stomach. There was no way of knowing how deeply it had traveled into his body, but when he tried to pull it out, it broke off in his hands, leaving most of it lodged above his trousers. The pain was oddly sharp and dull at the same time, leaving him weak and dizzy. He fell to his knees, blinking hard, fighting for consciousness, unaware of the gun that rattled to the floor by his side.

The last thing he saw before blackness clouded his eyes was Jose's face peering into his own. "*Muerte, hijo de puta,*" Jose said calmly. He waited until the deputy's eyes had glazed over and his jaw slackened. Then he walked slowly out of the shed.

Marta was waiting, cold and shivering a few feet away from the door. When she saw Jose emerge from the building, she ran to his side. "Don't go in there," he warned. She saw the look on his face. They stood motionless for some time, immobilized by fear.

It was Marta who first saw the smoke, and

160

realized its cause. It billowed out, at first in thin gray clouds, then in ever-increasing streams that threaded up through the trees. Bowles' cigarette, tossed away in the melee, had ignited the dry and brittle floorboards, compounded by the lack of moisture that had plagued the forest for several years. As soon as Marta saw the smoke, the flames began licking at the weak baseboards of the shed. Soon they had spread across the entire wall. Jose and Marta were scrambling up to the highway when the shed was engulfed, taking Bowles with it.

Chapter Twenty

At first Helen couldn't understand why she'd
woken up. There was nothing unusual going on in
the room. The lights were still on, Frieda was sound
asleep in a chair where she'd insisted on staying
when Helen lay down on the bed with a book. The
book had fallen off the bed onto the floor where it
lay splayed in a pool of light from the lamp. Helen
was looking at Frieda, thinking she should rouse her
from her cramped position on the chair to join her
in bed, when she recognized the acrid sting in her
nostrils.

Initially she couldn't believe it was a fire. Maybe someone was smoking a cigarette as he or she went by in the hall. She sat up on the bed and listened. No sound at all except for Frieda's shallow breathing. Helen glanced at her watch. Not yet eleven.

Luckily she was still dressed. She swung her legs off the bed. It felt odd to be walking around in that unnatural silence. Treading softly, Helen opened the door and slid out into the hallway.

Going down the stairs to the lobby, Helen was struck by the quiet — as if all the life had been drained out of the place by the awful scene that had occurred there earlier. No one was at the registration desk — surely that wasn't unusual. Downstairs, though, the smell of smoke was stronger.

As she stood, still a little dazed from sleep, in the middle of the lobby, Benson burst into the room, the doors gaping open behind him. A strange heat followed him. Helen looked into his round face. Dread grew inside her. He was shiny with sweat, and his eyes, so like his daughter's, gleamed with fear. Benson stared at her as if entranced, then stumbled by, bumping into the sofa and nearly toppling over one of the fake plants.

There was no doubt in Helen now. "Where? Benson, where is the fire?"

He was hanging onto the desk, breathing heavily. "Already called the fire department," he managed to get out. "It's right outside."

Helen stared at him in horror, then hurried to look for herself. Across the paved entrance, high above the treetops, she could see an orange glow that ebbed and flooded the sky, like an eerie tidal wave. Wisps of smoke floated up through the luminous wave, lit from underneath into grayish white shimmering shapes that flecked the black sky in swirling patterns. She could hear it now, too — a dull roar punctuated by crackling as branches and trees were consumed by destruction.

Helen fought for control as she ran back to Benson. "Come on, we've got to get everyone out of here." When he stared at her blankly she had to resist hitting him across his flaccid face. She grabbed him by the shoulders and shook him once, twice, violently. "Benson!" she cried, nearly shrieking. "Snap out of it!"

"What is it, Helen?" Frieda was somehow standing at her side, looking from Helen to Benson with eyes widened in fear. Helen let go of Benson. "We've got to get everyone out of here."

"But what —"

"Fire. Headed this way." Helen was already up the stairs. "You check out the first floor — maybe just Miranda down here. Get them out and waiting in the parking area. Benson said he already called the fire department." Frieda was gone before she had finished talking.

Helen raced down the hallway of the second floor, pounding on doors. Her yelling made enough commotion to waken everyone. Thanking whatever deities might be listening, Helen was grateful that the hotel had only two floors. Its attempt to be exclusive and minimize the number of guests would be a tremendous help tonight.

Mrs. McKendrick shrieked, put her hands to her face as if to block out the horror as her children clung to her, confused, made even more frightened by her behavior. Helen bodily grabbed her and shoved her in the direction of the stairway. "Get out to the parking area. The fire department should be here any second," she called after them, praying she was telling the truth.

Chester and Louise Palmer were clutching at each other and moaning. Chester held Louise by the arm and tried to guide her steps, but Louise was fainting as they went. Helen took her other arm and they half-dragged, half-walked the older woman down the stairs. Inwardly Helen cursed Louise for slowing down their progress. Every moment counted in getting to safety. As they rounded the corner of the stairs, Helen put out one hand to steady herself, her palm touching the wall for a fraction of a second. She might have imagined it, but she was almost sure that the building itself was warmer — the fire must be nearly there.

By the time they reached the lobby, Helen was hauling them after her. Chester stopped in his tracks, hyperventilating. Helen yanked harder to pull Louise along, and Chester tumbled behind. As they passed the counter, Helen saw with immense relief that Benson was no longer there. Frieda must have taken him outside with the rest. Heat billowed out at them when they passed through the front door, and the smoke was now a tangible presence.

"There they are!" The onrush of air had roused Chester from his stupor, and his bony finger pointed out the group huddled like a pack of animals in the center of the parking lot. Helen let the older couple go, and quickly counted heads. There was Frieda, trying to look calm. Amy and Alex, still maintaining a good bit of distance. The Palmers lurched to the

165

edge of the group. Mrs. McKendrick was squatting on the ground, babbling and crying as she rocked back and forth. Her children stood uncertainly beside her, hardly knowing which to fear most — the fire or their mother's panic.

Helen realized with a shock that stopped her cold that one of their number was missing. "Where's Miranda? Benson, where's your daughter?"

He was standing alone, at the edge of the parking lot, staring into the trees which were now laced through with light. He turned to look at her. "I already sent her on ahead," he said in a blank voice. "As soon as I called the fire department, so she could lead them on up here."

A loud shriek welled up from Mrs. McKendrick. Bobby and Susie, not sure what was happening, joined their voices to hers. Helen looked in the direction she was pointing. High above their heads, at the point where the paved surroundings of the hotel ended and the forest began, one tree towered over the others. Somehow — either by means of a flying spark, or, worse, because the fire had already reached that part of the woods — it had caught fire and was now a huge torch, looming up into the night sky. Branches snapped and fell with a swift crackle, and the trunk emitted weird, high-pitched noises as it was devoured.

"Look!" Frieda shouted. She gestured in the opposite direction, down the incline that hid the main road from view. Flashing red lights and the tinny wail of a siren filled Helen with immense relief. "Thank God, they're coming," she whispered. Chester and Louise clung to each other in tears, while the McKendrick children tried to get their mother to stop wailing. Even Amy and Alex took a couple of steps nearer to each other.

Helen stayed with Benson. His face didn't change expression. Filled with foreboding, again she asked him, "Where's Miranda, Benson? Come on, there's no time."

"I told you," he answered in a monotone. His eyes flickered as he stared past Helen's head, then the air was filled with a resounding boom that threatened to deafen everyone assembled there. The tree they had watched going up in flames shifted, sinking slightly, then fell over in slow motion, hitting the ground with a stunning blow that caused tremors.

"Jesus Christ," Helen murmured. She saw the flames start licking up whatever stood between the trees and the thin line of greenery that edged the parking lot. There was no time left. "Benson, if you're lying about Miranda . . ."

He turned away and joined the others. Frieda read Helen's expression and said, "It's blocking the road. We're trapped."

"And the fire engine can't get through. Oh, God, we're all going to die!" Mrs. McKendrick got to her feet and seemed to see for the first time that her children were standing there.

"The lake," Helen said. They all looked at her. "Come on, we can get to the water! In the boats! We can cross over to the other side, bypass the fire completely. Then we'll be able to get back down the road. If we stay here —" She broke off. She didn't have to complete her sentence.

"She's right," Frieda said. She was already ushering the rest of them to the path that led to the water. Before they could get out of the parking lot, the fire had spread nearly to the front doors of the hotel. The wave of heat advanced rapidly toward them, and smoke began to sear at their lungs. Helen saw that Benson seemed to be faring worse than the others — he went slowly, bending over frequently to pant for breath. She kept blinking, troubled by the strange sensation in her eyes. Then she realized she was feeling ashes as they sifted through the air.

By the time they had all gotten onto the path the hotel building itself was just beginning to catch fire. Helen shouldered her way to the front of the party to be next to Frieda. "We don't have long before these trees go up," she said in an undertone.

"I know. Maybe if we can just get everyone into the boats we'll be okay," Frieda answered. Suddenly they broke through to the sand, and they all breathed a sigh of relief at the cool wind blowing off the water. While they caught their breath, Helen strained her eyes in the darkness to find the boats. She ran out onto the tiny pier, her feet clattering loudly in the silence of the lake. "Only two boats," she breathed.

Alex had recovered his poise enough to join her on the pier. "Two," he said, echoing her thoughts. He glanced back at Amy, who was watching them.

"We'll have to do this in relays, we don't have any time to lose." She hurried back to the sand. The others gathered around, waiting for instructions. For just one second Helen felt like screaming at them to do something, to save themselves — quit looking at her for guidance. But she fought down her anger and spoke.

"We'll have to take turns in these boats, row

across the water and try to get back up to the main road on the other side of the lake."

They all stared at her, their upturned faces reminding her of children.

"God damn it, move!" Helen shouted.

Frieda stepped onto the pier first, then the others followed. Nobody questioned the McKendricks as they scrambled first into one of the boats. Chester and Louise came next, slowly and painfully, tottering. The vessel bobbed under their collective weight, listed wildly, then straightened out. Chester picked up an oar and urged Mrs. McKendrick to take the other one. Having something to do seemed to calm the hysterical woman, and soon the boat edged away from the pier and became a small white dot on the black water.

That left the O'Neills, Helen and Frieda standing on the pier with Benson. "All right, we don't have to argue about this," Alex said in a shaky voice. He tried to make a joke of it. "I feel like I'm on the Titanic. Women and children first." And he gave his wife a rough shove on the shoulders.

"Both of you, then," Helen said. She pulled Amy out onto the pier and forced her down into the boat. "We'll have plenty of time. Alex, you go with her. I don't think she can handle that boat by herself, and you'll need to go fast if you're going to get back here for the rest of us." She stared him down until Alex's gaze finally fell. He set his thick jaw firmly, to avoid looking humiliated, and stepped into the boat.

"You too, Frieda," Helen said.

"No, I'm staying here."

"Quit arguing with me, we can fight about it later." With one movement she picked up her love, feeling for the millionth time how slight she was, and lifted her into the boat. Then, not caring who saw her, Helen leaned over and kissed her on the cheek. She stood up and said in a husky voice, "Get going. You'll have to hurry."

"We will."

Helen heard the tears thick in Frieda's voice, so she looked away.

Alex had untied the rope and was wielding the oar awkwardly. "I'll be back in just a few minutes," he called over his shoulder. Helen and Benson watched the canoe drift away, and Helen stared at Frieda's white, terrified face until she could no longer make out the familiar features. The boat rode dangerously low in the water. It had been built for two, and the added weight of Alex in its center dipped it forward in the water. Soon, however, the canoe caught up with the rowboat, and the two vessels shrank under the gaze of the man and woman left behind.

There was a loud explosion. Helen and Benson turned in unison to see one of the largest towering pines near the lodge bend, topple and dissolve in a flash of sparks and smoke. Soon the other trees would catch fire. They looked at each other and read the same thought in their eyes. "Miranda," Benson breathed. Helen knew then that the worst was true — the girl had never left.

"Alex won't make it back for a few minutes yet," Helen said. "Let's go back up the path a ways. She's bound to be right there." She glanced at her companion and saw that his face was smooth and expressionless under the dirty streaks. His calm disturbed her, and then she saw that he was crying.

"Gone. Everything up in smoke." He spoke in a flat voice. Helen walked silently with him up the path, praying that Miranda would be there. Then she heard loud crackling noises and looked up to see the tops of the trees just ahead flickering into flame.

Suddenly on the path above them a figure emerged from the inferno. All at once the fire gathered momentum, and the trees behind Miranda became, as if by magic, flaming towers.

The acrid sting of smoke was in Helen's mouth and eyes, and soft gray ash settled onto her skin. The air was thick and cloudy around her. Helen fixed her eyes on Miranda and shouted as loud as her stinging lungs would allow. "Here! Over here! She waved her arms over her head at the girl. Benson stood immobile at her side, his eyes blankly staring. Helen glanced at him once and saw that he was too terrified to move. Maybe he hadn't even seen his daughter.

Miranda seemed to be looking straight at them, but Helen doubted if she could see or hear them. One moment she was there, the next she was gone, faded into the smoke. Then Helen couldn't breathe anymore. It was as if some huge piece of hot metal had wedged itself into her chest, collapsing her lungs like tired balloons. Her eyes flooded with tears and then darkened. She was convinced at that moment that death was coming. If only this awful pain and heat would end, she would welcome it. That was her last conscious thought.

An eternity later she heard voices. Men's voices. Who were they, why were they bothering her now? She felt herself being lifted up and over, then down into something. It was long and narrow, and it kept

171

moving. They were on the water. Slowly her brain began to clear and she tried to open her eyes. "She'll be all right, I think," Helen heard.

It hurt too much to open her eyes, so Helen lay back and breathed in the cold air. That hurt, too. Later she realized that she must have been drifting in and out of consciousness as they sailed across the lake. The next thing she knew was Frieda's arms bundling her into a scratchy blanket. Finally she was able to open her eyes.

"Oh, Helen, we're all right, you're all right." Frieda was laughing and crying all at once.

"Frieda," Helen tried to say, her throat rasping the sound painfully.

"Don't try to talk. They're taking us away now, to someplace safe."

But she had to talk, to ask the question. "Miranda?" she managed to get out.

Frieda shook her head and turned away, glancing over at the man standing next to Helen. Benson. Helen took one look at his face, then closed her eyes again. In another moment, the air was filled with sound — sirens, loud frantic voices, equipment and machinery rolling back and forth. Helen let herself sink back into darkness.

Chapter Twenty-One

When Helen stirred herself at last to look for Benson, the moon was high overhead. Unmoved and remote, it stared in the huge window of the clinic commandeered by the firefighters several hours ago. By the talk of those around her, Helen had taken in the fact that the blaze was now under control. The biggest danger in the eyes of the authorities — that the fire would spread down through Tilden Park and into Berkeley — had been averted. Now it was just a matter of controlling where it burned by Still

Waters Lake, letting it exhaust itself and collapse, spent, into a heap of ashen nothingness.

Much of the recent past was a blur for Helen. She remembered paramedics and the Red Cross workers hustling all around, calling out important-sounding commands and requests, squawking at each other over radios. She remembered Frieda's eyes, looming up at her from out of nowhere. She remembered the immense well of silence surrounding Benson when everyone realized just how enormous his loss had been.

Helen moved, for the first time in hours, carefully testing each sore, cramped muscle as she stood. Her throat and lungs were still parched. Each breath made her wince, but she was determined to find Benson and grateful that Frieda was not in sight. She picked up sounds as she moved through the dark hallway — the McKendrick family sleeping in a morass of blankets and muffled snores in one of the siderooms, Chester and Louise muttering and squirming under blankets on pallets at the other end of the hall.

With a start Helen saw Frieda flat on her back on a pallet next to Louise, one arm thrown up across her face as if warding off an expected blow. Slipping her own blanket off her shoulders, Helen stooped down to arrange it over Frieda. She lingered a moment, watching her lover sleep, then she reached out to touch her cheek. The skin was warm — maybe a slight fever — but her breathing was regular. Helen crept away quietly.

She found Benson sitting in a straight-backed chair just around the corner. The hall was deserted except for the man slouched before her. Helen found another chair and moved it next to him. They sat for a few minutes in an odd, silent companionship born of pain and exhaustion.

Benson spoke first. "We're going to be all right," he said tonelessly. "The doctors checked us all out. Nothing major."

"What about you?" Helen asked, swallowing painfully. God, she still hurt everywhere.

Benson shrugged and cleared his throat. "It doesn't matter. Nothing matters anymore." He ran his hand over his face in a shadow of a familiar gesture. "The hotel, Miranda —" His voice broke.

"You knew she was still there, didn't you? You were lying when you said she'd already left the hotel for the night."

Benson turned stiffly in his chair to look at her, his face more confused than angry. He finally said, "I don't know what you're talking about."

Helen looked out the window, trying to decide if she should go on. Outside, in the normal world, cars were passing by. People walked on the sidewalk, some of them staring curiously into the windows, hoping to get a glimpse of the victims, as if that would reassure them of their own safety. She said quietly, "I know that Miranda was at the hotel the night Jill died."

"She was at her sister's place in Oakland. Just like she said."

Benson's breathing was heavier now, but Helen pushed on, determined to tell the truth to someone. "Tell you what, Benson. You don't have to say a damn thing. You just have to listen."

"Why should I? For God's sake —"

"Because I have to know. If I can tell it to you,

then I'll know. Look, I have no proof. There's no way I can ever do anything about any of this."

As soon as she'd spoken, Helen regretted her words. Benson seemed to crumple in the chair beside her, shrinking down into his huge frame like a wilted plant. His eyes glittered at her but he said nothing.

She got up to go. "Never mind," she muttered. Then she felt a claw-like hand take her own. Her skin hurt to the touch, seared by heat as it was, and she nearly cried out.

"You started this," Benson said as she sank back into her chair. "You may as well go all the way, now."

"Are you sure?"

"Just start talking."

They sat side by side, in silence, staring out at the street.

"The first day at the hotel," Helen finally began, "Miranda let slip a remark that I'd nearly forgotten. A remark that told me she'd been here on Saturday night. We met on the rocks where Jill fell. It was the morning Miranda got back from Oakland —"

"She was out there? But I thought —"

"What?"

"Nothing. Go on." Benson stared straight ahead again, so Helen continued.

"She talked a lot about you — about the hotel, about some of the rough times Still Waters was having. And she told me about Jill. How they'd met in Mexico. I don't think she would have said a thing to me if it hadn't shaken her up quite a bit to see the spot where . . . where it happened. Maybe for the first time she realized what she'd done. She *is* an adolescent, with all the passion, all the irrational intensity adolescents face. I don't think it was real for her up until that moment."

Benson didn't ask what his daughter had done. He said, almost conversationally, "And just what did she say to you?"

"She mentioned how the water had been cut off that past weekend. If she'd gone away hours before that happened, how would she have known anything about it? Yet she was talking about it to me, before she'd even gone up to the hotel."

"I see." Benson heaved a deep sigh, which seemed to relax him. His face was expressionless. "Go on. Tell me the rest."

Helen looked at him uncertainly. "Well, other things added up, too. When we first arrived, Mrs. Palmer —"

"That fool. Should have left her to burn up."

"Mrs. Palmer was complaining about her towels not being outside the door on Sunday morning, although she'd called down to Marta — so she thought — and Marta had answered. In Spanish. But Miranda spoke Spanish fluently."

"So?"

"So what I think happened is that it was actually Miranda that Mrs. Palmer spoke with. It was after midnight and Miranda must have come back to the hotel, maybe to get cleaned up after going through the woods. When she discovered there was no water she went to the kitchen to wipe herself off, probably with the towels Marta had set aside for the Palmers. Miranda spoke briefly to Mrs.

177

Palmer, pretending to be Marta, then she drove out to Oakland, to her sister's house, and waited out the weekend."

Benson nodded sagely. "Okay. You still haven't said the most important thing. Motive. Why the hell —" He got up and stood in front of Helen, his voice shaking with anger, but still quiet, "— would my daughter go out of her way to kill a two-bit drunk who claimed to be a reporter but was no better than a junkie? Tell me that, you goddam bitch."

Helen looked back at him calmly. "Because Miranda was in love with Jill Gallagher."

Benson raised one hand as if to slap her and stopped himself. He breathed a curse but Helen saw his shaking body, heard the tremble in his voice as he said, "How dare you say such a thing about my little girl?"

"Because it's true, and you know it," Helen answered. "That night Miranda thought Jill was going to meet another lover. She followed her into the woods near the hotel."

"The woods?"

"Jill was doing something else out there. She wasn't meeting anyone, but Miranda didn't know that. I can't be sure, but I think Miranda probably took Jill's car keys and threw them into the forest — that way she'd have a better chance of talking to her because Jill couldn't shut herself in her car and drive away. Maybe she confronted Jill out there, maybe just followed her. Whatever it was, Jill broke away and got to the Lame Duck Saloon on foot. It was then that she decided to call me." Helen left out everything about the shed and Father John. Benson didn't need to know about that.

"Why would she call you? What did you have to do with it?"

"Because she knew she was in trouble. Miranda must have scared her, out there in the woods."

And she was afraid Miranda would get in the way of her story, Helen had to admit to herself. The story had come first — before Amy, before Miranda, before the safety of people like Marta and Jose — before everything.

"When she left the bar, Miranda followed her."

Helen stopped there. It was pointless to go on, to force the series of events to their bitter end. Benson leaned against the wall and stared down at her. His weight sagged against his arm, and Helen caught an acrid whiff of his stale sweat and the scorched cloth of his shirt.

Then Helen thought of something else. "I think it must have been Miranda who put Mrs. Palmer's wallet in Marta's bag, too. She wanted to discredit her, because Marta might have suspected something, since she knew she couldn't have been the one who'd spoken to Mrs. Palmer about the towels that night."

"Anything else?"

"Yes." Helen got up and stood beside him, unafraid. Their eyes were level, and she held his gaze. "You deliberately let her die. You knew she was in the hotel when the fire started, and you let it happen. Why?"

Helen was half-appalled, half-fascinated, at the cool way she was able to face a man who had done this monstrous act. Curiosity — could she dare to call it professional interest? — won out over disgust. If she was right, Benson had committed a horrifying crime — yet her desire to get at the truth overrode her shock.

Suddenly Benson wasn't listening anymore. He leaned against the wall and watched a panorama of memory unfolding in his mind. "Miranda was such a beautiful girl. It was a joy to watch her grow up. If only she'd been — like other girls her age. Wanting to get married, have some grandkids for us, spend her life with a good man."

"Instead of with people like Jill."

He sneered at her. "I know exactly what you are. It was all in that diary of hers, that notebook she kept. You, that woman you brought with you, that bitch Jill Gallagher. Miranda had already been corrupted by the reporter, down in Mexico. I learned that — I learned everything yesterday, in a diary I found of hers. Yes, she was an adolescent. But it was too late for her. She already had the sickness. The killing she did was part of the sickness." His lip curled in disgust and he leaned in closer. "If I had my way, all you perverts would have been burned in that fire."

"So you let Miranda be destroyed because she loved women."

"Because she was sick!" He turned away, folded his arms across his burly chest. "Don't preach to me — I won't listen. And you can't prove to anyone else one fucking word of what you're saying."

"To the police? No. But that doesn't matter now, Benson. You've already given me all the proof I need for what you did."

"What? What are you talking about?"

"The way you just sat there and listened to me. The only good things you could come up with about your own daughter had to do with her childhood — nothing about the person she was. You wouldn't give her the help she needed to understand herself. You'd prefer to remember her as your little girl, when she was safe and sound and untouched by the world. But she didn't stay that way, did she? And you couldn't forgive her for that."

"What the hell are you talking about? I loved that girl, with my whole heart." His voice broke and he began sobbing, tears streaming freely down his blackened cheeks.

"And yet you allowed her to die." Helen turned away, sickened, knowing there was nothing she could do about any of it. She had no proof, as she'd admitted to Benson. And now he would have to live with his deed for the rest of his life.

She could still hear his sobs echoing through the hall as she picked her way past chairs and pallets and stacks of blankets. Helen saw everything as if through thick glass, muffled, at an enormous distance. She still wasn't sure of what she had just done. How much of her work, her precious "career" as a detective, was based on cruelty? What purpose had been served by chasing down the truth if all it created was a lot of pain? Some sort of bridge had been crossed just now, and Helen wasn't too sure she liked where it led.

As soon as she turned the corner she saw Frieda waiting for her. Helen was too tired to think or feel any longer. She felt Frieda's breath on her neck. It was warm as she whispered, "Come on. Let's go home."

As they went back down the hall of the clinic, past the sleeping McKendricks, Helen looked up to see that the moon had gone down in a red and gold blaze of light. Soon the sun would be edging up over the hills. It was going to be a beautiful day.

Epilogue

Father John Hitchcock squinted as the early morning sunlight hit his face. The light streamed in through a window just opposite the desk in his study. The playground outside the church pealed with the laugher of children hurrying along the final few hours of the morning, eager for their lunch. The priest swung around in his chair, glanced up at Helen, then back down at the check he'd just removed from the envelope Helen had handed him.

To cover his surprise, Helen looked around the room as if seeing it for the first time. By the light of day the place looked a lot less ominous than it had a few nights ago. Of course, at that time she'd just been attacked. Now, instead of small and cramped and full of dark corners and sharp edges, it looked exactly like what it was — an overstuffed office, comfortably disordered and stamped with the personality of the man seated at the desk.

When the priest continued his silence, Helen turned from her perusal of the books on the shelves beside her. "Something wrong?"

He shook his head. "Are you sure you can afford this much?" he asked, gesturing with the check in his hand.

Helen shrugged. "I know you'll put it to good use." He was studying her, and Helen held his gaze, as if there were some kind of challenge in the air.

She knew, without reference to a mirror, what she must look like. The past week had not been kind to her. Every once in a while her throat still caught with the sting of the smoke she'd breathed in. Her dreams had been haunted by images of flames, of singed flesh, of piercing screams that ripped her back into consciousness. The bruises were beginning to fade from her face and neck, but there were one or two deep gashes on her legs, caused from running through the flaming brush, that would probably leave traces for months, perhaps years, to come. Even turning her head to face Father John was an effort that left her stiff and sore. Was it just the years catching up with her that made her feel so ragged, so aged by these events? Or was something else going on beneath the surface, something she didn't want to face? Something telling her it was time for a breather?

She laughed at the concern in his stare. "Is it that bad? I guess I look like the walking wounded."

He smiled back at her, and for the first time she noticed how kind his face was, now that it was no longer strained by fear and anger. The wrinkles gathered at the eyes and corners of the mouth told of many years of smiles and laughter. Rage was not his normal state.

"You look like you could use a few weeks off," he admitted. He replaced the check in the envelope with care, as if he were handling something very precious, then set it down gently in the top drawer of the desk. "I can't tell you how much this will mean to our work," he said as he closed the drawer. "It's incredibly generous on your part. I have to say . . ." He hesitated.

"What?"

"Well, I'm surprised to see you. The last time we met here things weren't exactly conducive to, shall we say, cordiality. Then at the hotel, when the deputy was taking Marta away —" He broke off, shook his head as if that would clear it of unpleasant memories. "I wonder if you happen to know —"

"Yes?"

He looked at her uncertainly, then back down at his hands drumming insistently on the desk. "Did anyone ever find out what happened to that man? With your friends in the police department, I thought you might have heard something."

Suddenly restless, Helen got up and began to roam around the tiny room. She stood by one of the narrow windows, watching the kids play basketball. A few chased one another out on the grass,

185

squealing with delight, none of them more than eight or nine years old. Three women stood on the strip of pavement that lined the school building, two of them wearing veils, the other with her short curly dark hair lifting and blowing in the mild spring breeze. Nuns, probably, Helen thought. They must be teachers here.

She felt with a rush how alien she was to this whole world — not just to the world of the Catholic church, which she'd been brought up to distrust along with Republicans and Yankees and foreigners. Standing there in the grubby study that bespoke a lifetime of caring, of commitment, she saw clearly her own rootlessness. It was an inability to attach herself to anything or anyone that she felt as an almost palpable part of herself. The only thing that she had felt committed to in the past couple of years had been work, and now she wasn't so sure about that either. Helen knew better than to blame herself for the events at Still Waters Lodge, but she also knew that her own actions had played some role in the outcome.

She felt his eyes on her, and answered him without turning from the window and the sight of the children playing, the nuns chatting. "The only piece of information I have is that human remains were found in the shed you had been using. So far no identification has been made, but Bowles was the only person in the vicinity of the hotel that night who's still unaccounted for." She didn't add that Miranda's body had been located almost immediately.

"I see."

She finally turned to look at him, and saw from his face that he probably did see, quite well.

She asked, "How are Marta and Jose? Don't worry, I'm not trying to find out where they are — I just want to know if they're all right," she hastened to add.

He smiled. "It's okay, I know that. They're doing fine. Started a new life in a new place. Hopefully they'll be able to stay there for a good long time."

"You mean they might have to pull up and go away again?"

"It happens. I think we covered our tracks pretty well this time, but you never know. Still, anything is better than what they were facing in El Salvador."

Helen sat down again. "Did they ever tell you anything about the night of the fire? What happened to Marta?"

He shook his head and avoided her glance. "Nothing. I guess we've all assumed that they got separated when the fire began, and the rest is history. Why?" His eyes clouded over with suspicion.

"Oh, it's nothing. I'm still trying to piece everything together for myself. It's all such a mess in my head, still. Probably always will be."

She was silent for a moment, unsure of how to say what she wanted to say, while he sat waiting. "Tell me, Father," she started with a humorous lilt in her voice, "do you have to be a Catholic to make confessions? Or can you hear one from anyone, including a deep-dyed Protestant?"

Relieved at her question, he laughed. "Well, technically only a Catholic can make a confession. But, as you've figured out, I don't get too hung up with technicalities." He smiled at her, encouraging her to go on.

She looked up at him and opened her mouth to

speak. Her eyes were caught by something she hadn't seen before — the unusual crucifix on the wall behind his head. The body of Jesus wasn't hung on wood, but suspended, arms outstretched, as if hanging lightly in the air. The expression, which she could read even from a distance, was serene and gentle. There was no blood, no bruises, no broken bones — just the torso clothed in a plain tunic. The eyes looked outward, as if seeing something far beyond the reach of human vision.

"Is there something you want to talk about, Helen?" It was the first time he'd used her name. The voice was quiet, as if afraid of scaring her off.

The moment passed. A bell rang, summoning the children and their teachers back to the classroom. Its normal sound seemed to snap something in Helen, and she felt her shell closing in again. "No, just curious. You know, where I grew up we were told that Catholics paid priests for absolution."

He laughed again, allowing the spell to be broken. "Well, then I've been ripped off all these years. It certainly hasn't made me any richer." Suddenly he leaned forward in the chair, spreading his palms flat on the desk in a gesture of openness. "Have you ever thought about getting involved in our work, Helen?"

Her eyes widened in surprise. "You mean — the refugees."

"Don't look so shocked. We could use someone like you. You're quick on your feet, you've been around — and I think that underneath that carefully hardened exterior you like to display, you care a lot."

She dropped her eyes from the intensity of his

gaze. "I don't think I can," she said. "Right now the best I can do for you is that check you have sitting in your drawer. I don't — I can't commit myself. And I know it requires commitment.'"

He nodded, realizing that she was talking about more than dedication to a cause. "Keep us in mind, though," he said lightly, as if talking about a new job opportunity.

"I will." She got up to go, and was almost out the door when he called her back. He got up from behind the desk and rounded the room to stand by her side.

"Look, I can see you're going through something. I'm not pressuring you to tell me what happened last night — obviously something did. I just want you to know I'm here if you ever want to talk to someone. I'm really not so bad, once you get to know me —" He grinned. "Even though I am a papist."

"Thanks for the offer." Helen felt overwhelmed with embarrassment, and for just a moment she thought of staying, of telling him some of the thoughts that weighed on her mind like blocks of granite. "I may take you up on that one of these days. But someone is waiting for me outside — I really can't stay."

He moved aside to let her go, and she went back out through the church and into the sunlight.

Just across the street Frieda was sitting in her car, reading a newspaper. Helen froze on the wide steps that led down away from the church to the street. She stared at Frieda as if looking at a stranger. The long slender neck, the thin fingers that grasped the flimsy sheets, the dark eyes that stared so intensely, as she stared at everything that

189

absorbed her attention — the familiar features that never failed to fascinate and frighten Helen at the same time — all these things appeared to Helen suddenly so curious, so new and amazing.

Frieda moved to turn a page, then caught sight of Helen across the street, hesitating on the steps. Helen started walking toward her as the engine roared to life.

"Everything okay? You look a little funny." Frieda glanced at the rearview mirror and in a moment they were out on the street, heading for home.

"I feel a little funny." Helen leaned back on the seat and closed her eyes. "You didn't have to drive me around today. You're still packing, right?"

"No problem." She looked briefly at Helen. "You really do look a little green around the gills. Sure you want to go car shopping this afternoon? Maybe you ought to stay in bed."

"No, no, that's okay. I've got to get started, get an idea. Maybe a truck this time."

"Are you sure you want a used car? Surely the insurance money will be enough for a new one. I mean, your car was cremated in the fire — no way they could say it wasn't totaled."

Helen thought again of the check sitting in Father John's desk, knowing where at least half of her insurance refund would be going. "No, I think this time around I want a used car."

"Okay." Frieda shrugged, and the sun blinked into the car window. They rode in silence until Helen finally turned the radio on to break the awful quiet in the car.

* * * * *

The cold weather had finally broken. Russell
Street shone under the brilliant sunshine. Outside,
kids were trying out their bicycles — popping
wheelies, racing, scooting down the pavement and
magically avoiding skateboarders. The grownups were
meandering out in robes to pick up newspapers and
call bleary greetings to one another. Helen turned
away from the cheerful scene and surveyed the
remains of breakfast that were, as usual, waiting for
her attack. This time there were no frying pans or
waffle irons to scrub out, no tidbits of egg or cheese
or toast to feed to the cat. Just the single cereal
bowl containing the soggy detritus of Helen's solitary
meal. She pushed herself away from the window,
glad to quit looking at her neighbors enjoying
themselves, and lifted the bowl down to the floor.
Boobella mewed her gratitude and began licking up
the milk, purring her pleasure. The mug of cold
coffee was next. The contents were poured down the
sink, the empty cup placed on the drainboard where
it began to form a stain. As she stood at the sink,
Helen caught a glimpse of the packed suitcase
waiting down the hall by the front door. She turned
away quickly and sat down at the kitchen table to
await the inevitable.

She could hear Frieda moving in the bedroom.
Drawers slid open, then were shut. The closet door
squawked when she entered it one last time to make
sure she wasn't leaving behind anything of
importance. Then there was a quick visit to the
bathroom. The more Helen tried not to listen, the
louder each sound became — it was as if she were
moving around in Frieda's body, making final
preparations for leaving.

Helen made sure she was looking down at the morning paper when Frieda walked into the kitchen. "All set?" she asked in a level voice.

"I think so." Frieda sat down. Helen saw that she was wearing something new — wool slacks topped by a cashmere sweater in a rich shade of red that brought out the lights in her hair. Frieda reached down to pet Boobella, who arched her back upward as she licked the bowl. Her hand lingered to stroke the cat's head, fingering the ears.

"You'll be warm in those clothes."

"It's always cooler by the ocean. This place looks right out on the water."

"I know, you told me." Helen could have kicked herself for the petulant tone. She'd been determined to maintain a cool, serene front through all of this, revealing no crack or chink in the facade. "It sounds like a great place."

"I'll give you a call as soon as I'm settled. We could have dinner or something."

"Sure. Sounds good." Helen got up quickly from the table and went to fiddle with the coffee maker. The dials and buttons blurred in her vision and she nearly cried out when she burned her fingers on the heated glass of the pot. "I guess you'll be pretty busy for a while, Helen." Suddenly Frieda's hands were on her shoulders, massaging, caressing. "It'll be okay. It'll be good for both of us."

It was the gentle touch that did it. Helen shrugged her hands off. "You mean it will be good for you. I never said I wanted you to go away. That's entirely your decision."

"Please, Helen. Not this morning."

"Then when? I'm not going to get another chance.

Shit!" Helen walked back to the sink to run cold water over her sore fingers. "Fine. Go ahead. Enjoy yourself."

"This is not exactly a picnic for me, either. Remember that afternoon on the beach by the lake, Helen? Remember what you said about keeping your life separate from mine? Well, I'm giving you a chance to do that. I'm doing my damnedest to give you all the space you need." Helen stayed at the sink, her back turned to Frieda. "All right, Helen. Time for me to go."

Frieda started down the hall, stopped, then ran back to the kitchen. Her arms embraced Helen from behind, and her lips found Helen's throat. "Goodbye. I'll call you," she whispered.

Helen stayed at the sink for a few moments after she had gone, staring into the empty dishes piled there. Boobella, finished with her meal, rubbed against Helen's leg twice, then three times, then settled into a long session cleaning her already immaculate fur. She protested faintly when Helen picked her up and held her close, then resigned herself to being clutched for a while.

Finally Helen spoke. "Come on, kitty," she mumbled into the warm fur. "Time to clean up."

A few of the publications of
THE NAIAD PRESS, INC.
P.O. Box 10543 • Tallahassee, Florida 32302
Phone (904) 539-5965
Toll-Free Order Number: 1-800-533-1973
Mail orders welcome. Please include 15% postage.

FLASHPOINT by Katherine V. Forrest. 256 pp. Lesbian
blockbuster!   ISBN 1-56280-043-4 $22.95

CROSSWORDS by Penny Sumner. 256 pp. 2nd VictoriaCross
Mystery.   ISBN 1-56280-064-7   9.95

SWEET CHERRY WINE by Carol Schmidt. 240 pp. A novel of
suspense.   ISBN 1-56280-063-9   9.95

CERTAIN SMILES by Dorothy Tell. 160 pp. Erotic short stories
                                      ISBN 1-56280-066-3   9.95

EDITED OUT by Lisa Haddock. 224 pp. 1st Carmen Ramirez
Mystery.   ISBN 1-56280-077-9   9.95

WEDNESDAY NIGHTS by Camarin Grae. 288 pp. Sexy
adventure.   ISBN 1-56280-060-4   10.95

SMOKEY O by Celia Cohen. 176 pp. Relationships on the playing
field.   ISBN 1-56280-057-4   9.95

KATHLEEN O'DONALD by Penny Hayes. 256 pp. Rose and
Kathleen find each other and employment in 1909 NYC.
                                      ISBN 1-56280-070-1   9.95

STAYING HOME by Elisabeth Nonas. 256 pp. Molly and Alix
want a baby . . . or do they?   ISBN 1-56280-076-0   10.95

TRUE LOVE by Jennifer Fulton. 240 pp. Six lesbians searching for
love in all the "right" places.   ISBN 1-56280-035-3   9.95

GARDENIAS WHERE THERE ARE NONE by Molleen Zanger.
176 pp. Why is Melanie inextricably drawn to the old house?
                                      ISBN 1-56280-056-6   9.95

MICHAELA by Sarah Aldridge. 256 pp. A "Sarah Aldridge"
romance.   ISBN 1-56280-055-8   10.95

KEEPING SECRETS by Penny Mickelbury. 208 pp. A Gianna
Maglione Mystery. First in a series. ISBN 1-56280-052-3   9.95

THE ROMANTIC NAIAD edited by Katherine V. Forrest &
Barbara Grier. 336 pp. Love stories by Naiad Press authors.
                                      ISBN 1-56280-054-X   14.95

UNDER MY SKIN by Jaye Maiman. 336 pp. A Robin Miller
mystery. 3rd in a series.   ISBN 1-56280-049-3.   10.95

STAY TOONED by Rhonda Dicksion. 144 pp. Cartoons — 1st
collection since *Lesbian Survival Manual.*   ISBN 1-56280-045-0   9.95

CAR POOL by Karin Kallmaker. 272pp. Lesbians on wheels
and then some!   ISBN 1-56280-048-5   9.95

NOT TELLING MOTHER: STORIES FROM A LIFE by Diane
Salvatore. 176 pp. Her 3rd novel.   ISBN 1-56280-044-2   9.95

GOBLIN MARKET by Lauren Wright Douglas. 240pp. A Caitlin
Reece Mystery. 5th in a series.   ISBN 1-56280-047-7   9.95

LONG GOODBYES by Nikki Baker. 256 pp. A Virginia Kelly
mystery. 3rd in a series.   ISBN 1-56280-042-6   9.95

FRIENDS AND LOVERS by Jackie Calhoun. 224 pp. Mid-western
Lesbian lives and loves.   ISBN 1-56280-041-8   9.95

THE CAT CAME BACK by Hilary Mullins. 208 pp. Highly praised
Lesbian novel.   ISBN 1-56280-040-X   9.95

BEHIND CLOSED DOORS by Robbi Sommers. 192 pp. Hot, erotic
short stories.   ISBN 1-56280-039-6   9.95

CLAIRE OF THE MOON by Nicole Conn. 192 pp. See the movie —
read the book!   ISBN 1-56280-038-8   10.95

SILENT HEART by Claire McNab. 192 pp. Exotic Lesbian
romance.   ISBN 1-56280-036-1   9.95

HAPPY ENDINGS by Kate Brandt. 272 pp. Intimate conversations
with Lesbian authors.   ISBN 1-56280-050-7   10.95

THE SPY IN QUESTION by Amanda Kyle Williams. 256 pp. 4th
Madison McGuire.   ISBN 1-56280-037-X   9.95

SAVING GRACE by Jennifer Fulton. 240 pp. Adventure and
romantic entanglement.   ISBN 1-56280-051-5   9.95

THE YEAR SEVEN by Molleen Zanger. 208 pp. Women surviving
in a new world.   ISBN 1-56280-034-5   9.95

CURIOUS WINE by Katherine V. Forrest. 176 pp. Tenth
Anniversary Edition. The most popular contemporary Lesbian
love story.   ISBN 1-56280-053-1   9.95

CHAUTAUQUA by Catherine Ennis. 192 pp. Exciting, romantic
adventure.   ISBN 1-56280-032-9   9.95

A PROPER BURIAL by Pat Welch. 192 pp. A Helen Black
mystery. 3rd in a series.   ISBN 1-56280-033-7   9.95

SILVERLAKE HEAT: A Novel of Suspense by Carol Schmidt.
240 pp. Rhonda is as hot as Laney's dreams.   ISBN 1-56280-031-0   9.95

LOVE, ZENA BETH by Diane Salvatore. 224 pp. The most talked
about lesbian novel of the nineties!   ISBN 1-56280-030-2   9.95

A DOORYARD FULL OF FLOWERS by Isabel Miller. 160 pp.
Stories incl. 2 sequels to *Patience and Sarah.*   ISBN 1-56280-029-9   9.95

MURDER BY TRADITION by Katherine V. Forrest. 288 pp. A
Kate Delafield Mystery. 4th in a series.   ISBN 1-56280-002-7   9.95

THE EROTIC NAIAD edited by Katherine V. Forrest & Barbara Grier.
224 pp. Love stories by Naiad Press authors.   ISBN 1-56280-026-4   12.95

DEAD CERTAIN by Claire McNab. 224 pp. A Carol Ashton
mystery. 5th in a series.   ISBN 1-56280-027-2   9.95

CRAZY FOR LOVING by Jaye Maiman. 320 pp. A Robin Miller
mystery. 2nd in a series.   ISBN 1-56280-025-6   9.95

STONEHURST by Barbara Johnson. 176 pp. Passionate regency
romance.   ISBN 1-56280-024-8   9.95

INTRODUCING AMANDA VALENTINE by Rose Beecham.
256 pp. An Amanda Valentine Mystery. First in a series.
ISBN 1-56280-021-3   9.95

UNCERTAIN COMPANIONS by Robbi Sommers. 204 pp.
Steamy, erotic novel.   ISBN 1-56280-017-5   9.95

A TIGER'S HEART by Lauren W. Douglas. 240 pp. A Caitlin
Reece mystery. 4th in a series.   ISBN 1-56280-018-3   9.95

PAPERBACK ROMANCE by Karin Kallmaker. 256 pp. A
delicious romance.   ISBN 1-56280-019-1   9.95

MORTON RIVER VALLEY by Lee Lynch. 304 pp. Lee Lynch at
her best!   ISBN 1-56280-016-7   9.95

THE LAVENDER HOUSE MURDER by Nikki Baker. 224 pp. A
Virginia Kelly Mystery. 2nd in a series.   ISBN 1-56280-012-4   9.95

PASSION BAY by Jennifer Fulton. 224 pp. Passionate romance,
virgin beaches, tropical skies.   ISBN 1-56280-028-0   9.95

STICKS AND STONES by Jackie Calhoun. 208 pp. Contemporary
lesbian lives and loves.   ISBN 1-56280-020-5   9.95

DELIA IRONFOOT by Jeane Harris. 192 pp. Adventure for Delia
and Beth in the Utah mountains.   ISBN 1-56280-014-0   9.95

UNDER THE SOUTHERN CROSS by Claire McNab. 192 pp.
Romantic nights Down Under.   ISBN 1-56280-011-6   9.95

RIVERFINGER WOMEN by Elana Nachman/Dykewomon.
208 pp. Classic Lesbian/feminist novel.   ISBN 1-56280-013-2   8.95

A CERTAIN DISCONTENT by Cleve Boutell. 240 pp. A unique
coterie of women.   ISBN 1-56280-009-4   9.95

GRASSY FLATS by Penny Hayes. 256 pp. Lesbian romance in
the '30s.   ISBN 1-56280-010-8   9.95

A SINGULAR SPY by Amanda K. Williams. 192 pp. 3rd Madison
McGuire.   ISBN 1-56280-008-6   8.95

THE END OF APRIL by Penny Sumner. 240 pp. A Victoria Cross
Mystery. First in a series.   ISBN 1-56280-007-8   8.95

A FLIGHT OF ANGELS by Sarah Aldridge. 240 pp. Romance set at
the National Gallery of Art   ISBN 1-56280-001-9   9.95

HOUSTON TOWN by Deborah Powell. 208 pp. A Hollis Carpenter
mystery. Second in a series.   ISBN 1-56280-006-X   8.95

KISS AND TELL by Robbi Sommers. 192 pp. Scorching stories by
the author of *Pleasures*.   ISBN 1-56280-005-1   9.95

STILL WATERS by Pat Welch. 208 pp. A Helen Black mystery.
2nd in a series.   ISBN 0-941483-97-5   9.95

TO LOVE AGAIN by Evelyn Kennedy. 208 pp. Wildly
romantic love story.   ISBN 0-941483-85-1   9.95

IN THE GAME by Nikki Baker. 192 pp. A Virginia Kelly
mystery. First in a series.   ISBN 01-56280-004-3   9.95

AVALON by Mary Jane Jones. 256 pp. A Lesbian Arthurian
romance.   ISBN 0-941483-96-7   9.95

STRANDED by Camarin Grae. 320 pp. Entertaining, riveting
adventure.   ISBN 0-941483-99-1   9.95

THE DAUGHTERS OF ARTEMIS by Lauren Wright Douglas.
240 pp. A Caitlin Reece mystery. 3rd in a series.
                                         ISBN 0-941483-95-9   9.95

CLEARWATER by Catherine Ennis. 176 pp. Romantic secrets
of a small Louisiana town.   ISBN 0-941483-65-7   8.95

THE HALLELUJAH MURDERS by Dorothy Tell. 176 pp. A Poppy
Dillworth mystery. 2nd in a series.   ISBN 0-941483-88-6   8.95

ZETA BASE by Judith Alguire. 208 pp. Lesbian triangle
on a future Earth.   ISBN 0-941483-94-0   9.95

SECOND CHANCE by Jackie Calhoun. 256 pp. Contemporary
Lesbian lives and loves.   ISBN 0-941483-93-2   9.95

BENEDICTION by Diane Salvatore. 272 pp. Striking,
contemporary romantic novel.   ISBN 0-941483-90-8   9.95

CALLING RAIN by Karen Marie Christa Minns. 240 pp.
Spellbinding, erotic love story   ISBN 0-941483-87-8   9.95

BLACK IRIS by Jeane Harris. 192 pp. Caroline's hidden past . . .
                                         ISBN 0-941483-68-1   8.95

TOUCHWOOD by Karin Kallmaker. 240 pp. Loving, May/
December romance.   ISBN 0-941483-76-2   9.95

BAYOU CITY SECRETS by Deborah Powell. 224 pp. A Hollis
Carpenter mystery. First in a series.   ISBN 0-941483-91-6   9.95

COP OUT by Claire McNab. 208 pp. A Carol Ashton mystery.
4th in a series.   ISBN 0-941483-84-3   9.95

LODESTAR by Phyllis Horn. 224 pp. Romantic, fast-moving
adventure.   ISBN 0-941483-83-5   8.95

THE BEVERLY MALIBU by Katherine V. Forrest. 288 pp. A
Kate Delafield Mystery. 3rd in a series.   ISBN 0-941483-48-7   9.95

THAT OLD STUDEBAKER by Lee Lynch. 272 pp. Andy's affair
with Regina and her attachment to her beloved car.
                                    ISBN 0-941483-82-7   9.95

PASSION'S LEGACY by Lori Paige. 224 pp. Sarah is swept into
the arms of Augusta Pym in this delightful historical romance.
                                    ISBN 0-941483-81-9   8.95

THE PROVIDENCE FILE by Amanda Kyle Williams. 256 pp.
Second Madison McGuire   ISBN 0-941483-92-4   8.95

I LEFT MY HEART by Jaye Maiman. 320 pp. A Robin Miller
Mystery. First in a series.   ISBN 0-941483-72-X   9.95

THE PRICE OF SALT by Patricia Highsmith (writing as Claire
Morgan). 288 pp. Classic lesbian novel, first issued in 1952 . . .
acknowledged by its author under her own, very famous, name.
                                    ISBN 1-56280-003-5   9.95

SIDE BY SIDE by Isabel Miller. 256 pp. From beloved author of
Patience and Sarah.   ISBN 0-941483-77-0   9.95

STAYING POWER: LONG TERM LESBIAN COUPLES
by Susan E. Johnson. 352 pp. Joys of coupledom.
                                    ISBN 0-941-483-75-4   12.95

SLICK by Camarin Grae. 304 pp. Exotic, erotic adventure.
                                    ISBN 0-941483-74-6   9.95

NINTH LIFE by Lauren Wright Douglas. 256 pp. A Caitlin
Reece mystery. 2nd in a series.   ISBN 0-941483-50-9   8.95

PLAYERS by Robbi Sommers. 192 pp. Sizzling, erotic novel.
                                    ISBN 0-941483-73-8   9.95

MURDER AT RED ROOK RANCH by Dorothy Tell. 224 pp.
A Poppy Dillworth mystery. 1st in a series.   ISBN 0-941483-80-0   8.95

LESBIAN SURVIVAL MANUAL by Rhonda Dicksion.
112 pp. Cartoons!   ISBN 0-941483-71-1   8.95

A ROOM FULL OF WOMEN by Elisabeth Nonas. 256 pp.
Contemporary Lesbian lives.   ISBN 0-941483-69-X   9.95

PRIORITIES by Lynda Lyons 288 pp. Science fiction with
a twist.   ISBN 0-941483-66-5   8.95

THEME FOR DIVERSE INSTRUMENTS by Jane Rule. 208
pp. Powerful romantic lesbian stories.   ISBN 0-941483-63-0   8.95

LESBIAN QUERIES by Hertz & Ertman. 112 pp. The questions
you were too embarrassed to ask.   ISBN 0-941483-67-3   8.95

CLUB 12 by Amanda Kyle Williams. 288 pp. Espionage thriller
featuring a lesbian agent!   ISBN 0-941483-64-9   8.95

DEATH DOWN UNDER by Claire McNab. 240 pp. A Carol
Ashton mystery. 3rd in a series.   ISBN 0-941483-39-8   9.95

MONTANA FEATHERS by Penny Hayes. 256 pp. Vivian and
Elizabeth find love in frontier Montana.   ISBN 0-941483-61-4   8.95

CHESAPEAKE PROJECT by Phyllis Horn. 304 pp. Jessie &
Meredith in perilous adventure.   ISBN 0-941483-58-4   8.95

LIFESTYLES by Jackie Calhoun. 224 pp. Contemporary Lesbian
lives and loves.   ISBN 0-941483-57-6   9.95

VIRAGO by Karen Marie Christa Minns. 208 pp. Darsen has
chosen Ginny.   ISBN 0-941483-56-8   8.95

WILDERNESS TREK by Dorothy Tell. 192 pp. Six women on
vacation learning "new" skills.   ISBN 0-941483-60-6   8.95

MURDER BY THE BOOK by Pat Welch. 256 pp. A Helen
Black Mystery. First in a series.   ISBN 0-941483-59-2   9.95

LESBIANS IN GERMANY by Lillian Faderman & B. Eriksson.
128 pp. Fiction, poetry, essays.   ISBN 0-941483-62-2   8.95

THERE'S SOMETHING I'VE BEEN MEANING TO TELL
YOU Ed. by Loralee MacPike. 288 pp. Gay men and lesbians
coming out to their children.   ISBN 0-941483-44-4   9.95

LIFTING BELLY by Gertrude Stein. Ed. by Rebecca Mark. 104
pp. Erotic poetry.   ISBN 0-941483-51-7   8.95

ROSE PENSKI by Roz Perry. 192 pp. Adult lovers in a long-term
relationship.   ISBN 0-941483-37-1   8.95

AFTER THE FIRE by Jane Rule. 256 pp. Warm, human novel
by this incomparable author.   ISBN 0-941483-45-2   8.95

SUE SLATE, PRIVATE EYE by Lee Lynch. 176 pp. The gay
folk of Peacock Alley are all cats.   ISBN 0-941483-52-5   8.95

CHRIS by Randy Salem. 224 pp. Golden oldie. Handsome Chris
and her adventures.   ISBN 0-941483-42-8   8.95

THREE WOMEN by March Hastings. 232 pp. Golden oldie. A
triangle among wealthy sophisticates.   ISBN 0-941483-43-6   8.95

RICE AND BEANS by Valeria Taylor. 232 pp. Love and
romance on poverty row.   ISBN 0-941483-41-X   8.95

PLEASURES by Robbi Sommers. 204 pp. Unprecedented
eroticism.   ISBN 0-941483-49-5   8.95

EDGEWISE by Camarin Grae. 372 pp. Spellbinding
adventure.   ISBN 0-941483-19-3   9.95

FATAL REUNION by Claire McNab. 224 pp. A Carol Ashton
mystery. 2nd in a series.   ISBN 0-941483-40-1   8.95

KEEP TO ME STRANGER by Sarah Aldridge. 372 pp. Romance
set in a department store dynasty.   ISBN 0-941483-38-X   9.95

IN THE BLOOD by Lauren Wright Douglas. 252 pp. Lesbian
science fiction adventure fantasy   ISBN 0-941483-22-3   8.95

THE BEE'S KISS by Shirley Verel. 216 pp. Delicate, delicious
romance.   ISBN 0-941483-36-3   8.95

RAGING MOTHER MOUNTAIN by Pat Emmerson. 264 pp.
Furosa Firechild's adventures in Wonderland.   ISBN 0-941483-35-5   8.95

IN EVERY PORT by Karin Kallmaker. 228 pp. Jessica's sexy,
adventuresome travels.   ISBN 0-941483-37-7   9.95

OF LOVE AND GLORY by Evelyn Kennedy. 192 pp. Exciting
WWII romance.   ISBN 0-941483-32-0   8.95

CLICKING STONES by Nancy Tyler Glenn. 288 pp. Love
transcending time.   ISBN 0-941483-31-2   9.95

SURVIVING SISTERS by Gail Pass. 252 pp. Powerful love
story.   ISBN 0-941483-16-9   8.95

SOUTH OF THE LINE by Catherine Ennis. 216 pp. Civil War
adventure.   ISBN 0-941483-29-0   8.95

WOMAN PLUS WOMAN by Dolores Klaich. 300 pp. Supurb
Lesbian overview.   ISBN 0-941483-28-2   9.95

HEAVY GILT by Delores Klaich. 192 pp. Lesbian detective/
disappearing homophobes/upper class gay society.

                                            ISBN 0-941483-25-8   8.95

THE FINER GRAIN by Denise Ohio. 216 pp. Brilliant young
college lesbian novel.   ISBN 0-941483-11-8   8.95

HIGH CONTRAST by Jessie Lattimore. 264 pp. Women of the
Crystal Palace.   ISBN 0-941483-17-7   8.95

OCTOBER OBSESSION by Meredith More. Josie's rich, secret
Lesbian life.   ISBN 0-941483-18-5   8.95

BEFORE STONEWALL: THE MAKING OF A GAY AND
LESBIAN COMMUNITY by Andrea Weiss & Greta Schiller.
96 pp., 25 illus.   ISBN 0-941483-20-7   7.95

WE WALK THE BACK OF THE TIGER by Patricia A. Murphy.
192 pp. Romantic Lesbian novel/beginning women's movement.
                                            ISBN 0-941483-13-4   8.95

SUNDAY'S CHILD by Joyce Bright. 216 pp. Lesbian athletics, at
last the novel about sports.   ISBN 0-941483-12-6   8.95

OSTEN'S BAY by Zenobia N. Vole. 204 pp. Sizzling adventure
romance set on Bonaire.   ISBN 0-941483-15-0   8.95

LESSONS IN MURDER by Claire McNab. 216 pp. A Carol
Ashton mystery. First in a series.   ISBN 0-941483-14-2   9.95

YELLOWTHROAT by Penny Hayes. 240 pp. Margarita, bandit,
kidnaps Julia.   ISBN 0-941483-10-X   8.95

SAPPHISTRY: THE BOOK OF LESBIAN SEXUALITY by
Pat Califia. 3d edition, revised. 208 pp.   ISBN 0-941483-24-X   10.95

CHERISHED LOVE by Evelyn Kennedy. 192 pp. Erotic
Lesbian love story.   ISBN 0-941483-08-8   9.95

LAST SEPTEMBER by Helen R. Hull. 208 pp. Six stories & a
glorious novella.   ISBN 0-941483-09-6   8.95

THE SECRET IN THE BIRD by Camarin Grae. 312 pp. Striking,
psychological suspense novel.   ISBN 0-941483-05-3   8.95

TO THE LIGHTNING by Catherine Ennis. 208 pp. Romantic
Lesbian 'Robinson Crusoe' adventure.   ISBN 0-941483-06-1   8.95

THE OTHER SIDE OF VENUS by Shirley Verel. 224 pp.
Luminous, romantic love story.   ISBN 0-941483-07-X   8.95

DREAMS AND SWORDS by Katherine V. Forrest. 192 pp.
Romantic, erotic, imaginative stories.   ISBN 0-941483-03-7   8.95

MEMORY BOARD by Jane Rule. 336 pp. Memorable novel
about an aging Lesbian couple.   ISBN 0-941483-02-9   9.95

THE ALWAYS ANONYMOUS BEAST by Lauren Wright
Douglas. 224 pp. A Caitlin Reece mystery. First in a series.
                        ISBN 0-941483-04-5   8.95

DUSTY'S QUEEN OF HEARTS DINER by Lee Lynch. 240 pp.
Romantic blue-collar novel.   ISBN 0-941483-01-0   8.95

PARENTS MATTER by Ann Muller. 240 pp. Parents'
relationships with Lesbian daughters and gay sons.
                        ISBN 0-930044-91-6   9.95

MAGDALENA by Sarah Aldridge. 352 pp. Epic Lesbian novel
set on three continents.   ISBN 0-930044-99-1   8.95

THE BLACK AND WHITE OF IT by Ann Allen Shockley.
144 pp. Short stories.   ISBN 0-930044-96-7   7.95

SAY JESUS AND COME TO ME by Ann Allen Shockley. 288
pp. Contemporary romance.   ISBN 0-930044-98-3   8.95

LOVING HER by Ann Allen Shockley. 192 pp. Romantic love
story.   ISBN 0-930044-97-5   7.95

MURDER AT THE NIGHTWOOD BAR by Katherine V.
Forrest. 240 pp. A Kate Delafield mystery. Second in a series.
                        ISBN 0-930044-92-4   9.95

ZOE'S BOOK by Gail Pass. 224 pp. Passionate, obsessive love
story.   ISBN 0-930044-95-9   7.95

WINGED DANCER by Camarin Grae. 228 pp. Erotic Lesbian
adventure story.   ISBN 0-930044-88-6   8.95

PAZ by Camarin Grae. 336 pp. Romantic Lesbian adventurer
with the power to change the world.   ISBN 0-930044-89-4   8.95

SOUL SNATCHER by Camarin Grae. 224 pp. A puzzle, an
adventure, a mystery — Lesbian romance.   ISBN 0-930044-90-8   8.95

THE LOVE OF GOOD WOMEN by Isabel Miller. 224 pp.
Long-awaited new novel by the author of the beloved *Patience
and Sarah.*   ISBN 0-930044-81-9   8.95

THE HOUSE AT PELHAM FALLS by Brenda Weathers. 240
pp. Suspenseful Lesbian ghost story.   ISBN 0-930044-79-7   7.95

HOME IN YOUR HANDS by Lee Lynch. 240 pp. More stories
from the author of *Old Dyke Tales.*   ISBN 0-930044-80-0   7.95

SURPLUS by Sylvia Stevenson. 342 pp. A classic early Lesbian
novel.   ISBN 0-930044-78-9   7.95

PEMBROKE PARK by Michelle Martin. 256 pp. Derring-do
and daring romance in Regency England.   ISBN 0-930044-77-0   7.95

THE LONG TRAIL by Penny Hayes. 248 pp. Vivid adventures
of two women in love in the old west.   ISBN 0-930044-76-2   8.95

AN EMERGENCE OF GREEN by Katherine V. Forrest. 288
pp. Powerful novel of sexual discovery.   ISBN 0-930044-69-X   9.95

THE LESBIAN PERIODICALS INDEX edited by Claire
Potter. 432 pp. Author & subject index.   ISBN 0-930044-74-6   12.95

DESERT OF THE HEART by Jane Rule. 224 pp. A classic;
basis for the movie *Desert Hearts.*   ISBN 0-930044-73-8   9.95

FOR KEEPS by Elisabeth Nonas. 144 pp. Contemporary novel
about losing and finding love.   ISBN 0-930044-71-1   7.95

TORCHLIGHT TO VALHALLA by Gale Wilhelm. 128 pp.
Classic novel by a great Lesbian writer.   ISBN 0-930044-68-1   7.95

LESBIAN NUNS: BREAKING SILENCE edited by Rosemary
Curb and Nancy Manahan. 432 pp. Unprecedented autobiographies
of religious life.   ISBN 0-930044-62-2   9.95

THE SWASHBUCKLER by Lee Lynch. 288 pp. Colorful novel
set in Greenwich Village in the sixties.   ISBN 0-930044-66-5   8.95

MISFORTUNE'S FRIEND by Sarah Aldridge. 320 pp. Historical Lesbian novel set on two continents.   ISBN 0-930044-67-3   7.95

These are just a few of the many Naiad Press titles — we are the oldest and
largest lesbian/feminist publishing company in the world. Please request a
complete catalog. We offer personal service; we encourage and welcome direct
mail orders from individuals who have limited access to bookstores carrying
our publications.